RASMUS AND THE VAGABOND

When Rasmus ran away from his orphanage, he was determined to find parents to love him and a home of his own. But he was sorry to leave his friend Gunnar, and as he trudged along the unfriendly road, Rasmus grew more and more homesick for the only home he knew.

Then Rasmus met Paradise Oscar, a bighearted tramp who took Rasmus along on his travels. As the two wandered along the open road, they encountered danger and excitement, robbers and police. Rasmus loved the adventure in his new life, and he began to wish it would never end. Until one day Rasmus found something he wanted even more....

"Rasmus and Oscar are wonderful and distinctive characters, whom children will long remember. And a more satisfactory story than theirs, combining excitement and suspense, humor and pathos, would be hard to find." —*Chicago Tribune*

ASTRID LINDGREN

Rasmus
AND THE
Vagabond

TRANSLATED BY GERRY BOTHMER

ILLUSTRATED BY ERIC PALMQUIST

PUFFIN BOOKS

PUFFIN BOOKS
Viking Penguin Inc., 40 West 23rd Street, New York, New York 10010, U.S.A.
Penguin Books Ltd, 27 Wrights Lane, London W8 5TZ (Publishing & Editorial) and
Harmondsworth, Middlesex, England (Distribution & Warehouse)
Penguin Books Australia Ltd, Ringwood, Victoria, Australia
Penguin Books Canada Limited, 2801 John Street, Markham, Ontario, Canada L3R 1B4
Penguin Book (N.Z.) Ltd, 182-190 Wairau Road, Auckland 10, New Zealand

First published by The Viking Press 1960
Published in Puffin Books 1987
Copyright © Astrid Lindgren, 1960
All rights reserved
Printed in the United States of America by R. R. Donnelley & Sons Company,
Harrisonburg, Virginia
Set in Electra

Library of Congress Cataloging in Publication Data
Lindgren, Astrid, 1907–   . Rasmus and the vagabond.
Translation of: Rasmus på luffen.
Summary: After running away from the orphanage, nine-year-old Rasmus finds the outside
world cold and unfriendly until he meets "Paradise Oscar," who helps him find a new home.
[1. Orphans—fiction]   I. Palmquist, Eric, ill.   II. Title.
[PZ7.L6585Ras   1987]   [Fic]   86-30248   ISBN 0-14-032304-X

Contents

Rasmus and the Vagabond

1. The Lucky Day

Rasmus was sitting in his regular notch in the linden tree, thinking about things that shouldn't be allowed to exist. Potatoes were at the top of the list. Cooked, with gravy on them for Sunday dinner they were all right, but when they kept on sprouting in the field and had to be dug up—then they shouldn't be tolerated. He could also easily do without Miss Hawk, for it was she who was always saying, "Tomorrow we're going to spend the day digging up potatoes."

"We" she said, but of course that didn't include her. It was Rasmus and Gunnar and Big Peter and the other boys who had to slave in the potato field the whole hot summer day. To top it off, they had to watch the village kids troop by on their way to the swimming place down at the river! Snooty village kids—they shouldn't be allowed around either.

Rasmus was trying to think whether there was anything else he could put on his list to be done away with, but a hiss from below interrupted his deliberations.

"Rasmus! Hide! The Hawk is coming!"

Gunnar had popped his head out of the woodshed door, and Rasmus moved fast. He slipped away from his perch in the tree, and when Miss Hawk a second later stood outside the woodshed there was no Rasmus to be seen in the green branches of the linden. This was lucky for Rasmus because Miss Hawk strongly disapproved of boys' flitting about in trees like birds when there was useful work to be done.

"Gunnar, I hope you're only cutting the spruce wood?" Miss Hawk's steely eyes scrutinized the wood which Gunnar had gathered in the sack.

"Yes, Miss Hawk," said Gunnar in the tone of voice he was supposed to use when he answered Miss Hawk. It was the special orphanage voice they had to use when talking to the directress, or to the parson when he came on an inspection visit and asked them if they didn't think it was fun to work in the garden, or when one of the village children's parents came to complain that their boy had been beaten up for shouting "orphan" in the schoolyard. Then the orphanage children had to put all the gentleness and obedience they could muster into their voices because that is what was expected—by Miss Hawk and the parson and everybody.

"Do you know where Rasmus is?" said Miss Hawk.

Alarmed, Rasmus pressed himself still closer to the branch from which he was dangling and prayed that Miss Hawk would go away. He couldn't keep hanging on like this much longer. His arms were starting to ache. They would gradually give and he would sink down right in front of Miss Hawk. The blue-and-white-striped orphanage shirt he was wearing didn't help any either. The birds in the trees were so hard to spot because God had given them protective coloring, the teacher had said. But God hadn't provided orphan boys with protective coloring, and therefore Rasmus begged God with all his heart to send Miss Hawk away before he dropped.

It wasn't long since Miss Hawk had scolded him because he got himself dirtier than anyone else in the orphanage. But just wait! The next time she said anything like that he would just say that he was working on his protective coloring. But he would say it to himself, of course. You didn't say such things so that the Hawk heard them, because her eyes were so steely and her mouth was so hard, and sometimes the wrinkles in her forehead were so severe. Gunnar claimed that even her nose was severe, but Rasmus didn't agree. In fact, he thought that the Hawk had quite a nice

nose—although hanging in the tree in this agonizing position, his arms going to sleep, he could hardly think of anything nice about the Hawk.

Gunnar was trembling as he kept piling wood into the sack
while Miss Hawk stood by watching. He didn't even dare
raise his eyes as high as her nose. All he saw of her was a bit
of her stiffly starched apron.

"Do you know where Rasmus is?" Miss Hawk repeated
impatiently, since she hadn't received an answer to her first
question.

"I saw him a while ago over by the chicken coop," said
Gunnar. That was the honest-to-goodness truth. Half an
hour ago, Gunnar and Rasmus had been looking for eggs
in the nettles behind the chicken coop, where the silly hens
would sometimes sneak off to lay their eggs. So Gunnar *had*
seen Rasmus there. But his present whereabouts Gunnar
thought it would be better if Miss Hawk didn't know.

"If you see him, tell him that he has to pull up a basket-
ful of nettles," said Miss Hawk, abruptly turning on her
heels and leaving.

"Yes, Miss Hawk," said Gunnar.

"Did you hear that?" he said when Rasmus came climbing down from the linden tree. "You're to pull up a basket-
ful of nettles."

Nettles shouldn't be allowed to exist either, Rasmus
thought. All summer the boys had to pick nettles for the
hens, who ate them boiled every day.

"Can't those stupid hens eat the nettles when they grow
right under their beaks?"

"Of course they can't," said Gunnar. "They have to be served properly, if you please."

He made a deep bow to a hen who came strutting idly along, cackling.

Rasmus wasn't sure whether hens should be wiped out or not, but he finally decided in favor of letting them live. Without hens there wouldn't be eggs for Sunday breakfast and without eggs on Sunday it would be hard to tell what day it was. Since hens had to be, he might as well get to work and pull up those nettles.

Rasmus wasn't any lazier than any other nine-year-old. He just had a natural dislike of everything which kept him from climbing trees or swimming in the river or playing robbers with the other boys and lying in ambush behind the potato cellar when the girls would come to fetch potatoes. This was his idea of time well spent.

But it wasn't Miss Hawk's, and that was quite natural. Vaesterhaga Orphanage was a municipal institution which got part of its income by selling eggs and vegetables. The children were a cheap and necessary labor force, and Miss Hawk didn't put any inhuman demands on them, even if Rasmus considered it inhuman to make him dig up potatoes all day. But since he and the other orphans would have to support themselves when they reached the age of thirteen, it was necessary for them to learn to work. This was Miss Hawk's understanding, but unfortunately she did not understand how necessary it was for children even in an orphanage to play. But perhaps this was too much to expect, since she herself had never been very fond of playing.

Rasmus was obediently pulling up nettles behind the chicken coop, but as he worked he told the chickens what he thought of them.

"Lazy critters like you shouldn't be allowed. Nettles are growing around here like crazy, but no, that won't do. I have to work like a slave and pull them up for you."

The more he thought about it, the more he began to feel like a slave, and it was quite fun. Last term his teacher had read them a book about slavery in America a long time ago. He liked nothing better than to have the teacher read to them, and the book about slavery was the most exciting story Rasmus had ever heard.

He groaned as he pulled up the nettles because now he could feel the slave driver's whip on him and there were bloodhounds behind the ice house ready to attack him if he didn't fill the basket fast enough. It was American cotton he was picking now, not Swedish nettles. The big mitten he was wearing in order not to get a nettle burn was not exactly what one would expect a slave to be wearing under the burning southern sun, but he just couldn't do without it.

Rasmus tugged and pulled. But sometimes even slaves have nice things happen to them. Several enormous nettles were growing over by the ice house, and though by now Rasmus had his basket full, he went over and ripped them out just the same to tease the bloodhounds. Then, all of a sudden, his eye caught something lying in the sawdust next to the ice house. It was partly covered with sawdust but it looked quite a lot like a coin. Rasmus' heart beat faster. It couldn't be real money—such things didn't happen! But just the same he pulled off his mitten and stretched out his hand to grab it. It was a five-cent piece! The cotton fields vanished, the bloodhounds too, and the poor slave stood there dizzy, his head spinning with elation.

It seemed to Rasmus that five cents would buy just about anything he wanted—a big bag of candy or five pieces of toffee or a chocolate bar. Perhaps he could run down to the village candy store during lunch hour tomorrow. Or else he could hold on to the money in the happy thought that he was rich and could buy anything he wanted.

Now chickens should definitely be allowed, and nettles

too, because without chickens and nettles this would never have happened. He was sorry that he had been so unfriendly to the poor chickens a while ago. Judging by the way they were strutting around in the chicken coop, their feelings didn't seem to have been hurt too much. But he still wanted them to know that he didn't have anything against them.

"You certainly should be allowed to exist," he said as he walked over to the chicken coop. "I'm going to pull up nettles for you every day."

Then a new miracle happened. He saw another treasure! A sea-shell was lying at the feet of a cackling leghorn hen! Right in the middle of all the chicken dirt lay a beautiful white shell with small brown spots.

"Oh," said Rasmus. "Oh!"

He quickly unhooked the gate to the chicken coop and without paying the slightest attention to the wild scurrying in every direction he rushed in and grabbed the shell.

His delight was so great that he felt unable to bear it alone. He just had to tell Gunnar all about it—poor Gunnar, who had been with him at the chicken coop only an hour ago and hadn't found a shell or a five-cent piece! Rasmus became thoughtful. Perhaps neither the shell nor the coin had been there an hour ago. Perhaps they had got there by some sort of magic just when he began pulling up nettles. Maybe this was to be his lucky day when only fantastic things happened. He'd better ask Gunnar what he thought about it.

Rasmus started to run but suddenly stopped when he remembered the basket of nettles. He went back to the ice house to pick it up and, with the basket in one hand and the coin held tightly in the other, he ran to look for Gunnar.

He found him over at the playground where the children gathered when their work was over for the day. The whole group was together and everyone seemed tense and anxious. Something must have happened while Rasmus was away.

Rasmus was eager to get Gunnar off by himself and show him his treasures, but Gunnar had more important things to talk about.

"We're not going to dig up potatoes tomorrow," he informed Rasmus. "Some people are coming tomorrow to pick out a kid."

In the face of this news, the coin and the shell faded into the background. Nothing could be as important as the possibility that someone in the group would get a home of his own. There wasn't a child at Vaesterhaga who wasn't dreaming of that. Even the bigger boys and girls who would soon be ready to go out on their own hoped against all reason for such a miracle. Even the ugliest and most impossible of them wouldn't stop hoping that some day someone would come who for some strange, wonderful, unexplainable reason wanted just him or her, not as a servant to order around, but as their own child. To have parents was the greatest joy the children at the orphanage could imagine. Not all of them would admit their hopeless longing openly. But Rasmus was only nine and too young to hide his heart.

"Just think," he said eagerly, "if they should pick me! Oh how I wish that they would want me."

"Bah! Don't get any ideas," said Gunnar. "They always pick girls with curly hair."

Rasmus' spirits sank and an expression of black despair spread over his face. He looked pleadingly at Gunnar. "Don't you think there might be a chance that someone would want a boy with straight hair?"

"They want girls with curly hair, I told you."

Gunnar was an unusually homely boy with a pug nose and hair as coarse as a goat's. He kept his dreams and hopes of having a father and mother a deep secret. No one would ever have guessed that he cared in the least who would be chosen tomorrow.

Later, lying in his narrow bed beside Gunnar's in the boy's dormitory, Rasmus remembered that he still hadn't told him about the shell and the coin. He leaned over and whispered, "Gunnar, listen, so many strange things have happened today."

"What sort of strange things?" asked Gunnar.

"I found a five-cent piece and a beautiful shell, but don't tell anybody."

"Let me see," whispered Gunnar, who was now curious. "Come, let's go over to the window so I can see."

They tiptoed over to the window in their nightshirts, and in the clear light of the summer twilight Rasmus showed off his treasures, carefully so that no one could see.

"How lucky you are," said Gunnar, running his index finger over the smooth shell.

"Yes, I'm lucky. And because I am, the people who are coming tomorrow might want me."

"Listen to him!" scoffed Gunnar.

Big Peter, the oldest of the boys at the orphanage and self-appointed leader, was in the bed next to the door. He had raised himself on his elbow and was listening tensely.

"Get into bed," he whispered. "The Hawk is coming. I hear her clomping up the stairs."

Gunnar and Rasmus made a dash for their beds, their nightshirts flapping around their bare legs, and when the Hawk came into the dormitory you could have heard a pin drop.

The directress was making her nightly rounds, going from bed to bed to make sure everybody was settled down. Very rarely she would give one of the boys a reluctant pat on the head as she came by. Rasmus didn't like the Hawk, but every night he wished that she would stroke him—he didn't know why.

If she comes by and strokes me tonight, thought Rasmus as he lay there, it means that I'll have luck tomorrow too. It will mean that the people who are coming will want me, even though my hair is straight.

Now Miss Hawk was close to Gunnar's bed. Rasmus lay stiff with suspense. Now . . . now she would be coming to him.

"Rasmus, don't lie there picking holes in the blanket," was all she said.

Then she continued her inspection and in the next minute she had closed the door behind her, calmly, firmly, sternly. All was quiet in the dormitory, but from Rasmus came a deep sigh.

2. Disappointment

Lots of soap was used in the boys' washroom the next morning. Clean ears and scrubbed hands were the first things foster parents looked for, if you could believe the Hawk, and today everyone was anxious to put his best foot forward.

Rasmus grabbed a big piece of soap and started to scrub himself more thoroughly than he had since the day before Christmas Eve. He was a boy, and he did have straight hair —that couldn't be changed. But if it was only a question of the ears, he would show up with the cleanest ears in all of Vaesterhaga, and no one's hands would be redder from scrubbing than his. The girls had an advantage there too, for they were unnaturally clean. It seemed that dirt didn't stick to them in the same way that it did to boys. And besides, they were always doing dishes, scrubbing floors and baking and things like that, so they got clean without trying.

Big Peter was standing in the middle of the floor. He still hadn't touched his soap or his brush. He was going to be thirteen in the fall and he would have to leave Vaesterhaga whether he wanted to or not. He knew that he would have to start working as a farmhand for some farmer in the vicinity, and he also knew that, no matter how thoroughly he washed his ears, nothing could change that.

"I'm not going to wash today," he announced in a loud voice.

There was a sudden pause in the scrubbing at the basins. Big Peter was the leader and he wasn't going to wash. Now the problem was to decide what the rest of them were going to do.

"I'm not going to wash either," said Gunnar, putting his brush down with a bang. He was also aware that soap and water couldn't accomplish any miracles as far as his looks were concerned.

"Have you gone crazy?" asked Rasmus, pushing his wet hair out of his eyes. "You know who is coming."

"You seem to think that it's old King Oscar come back to life," said Gunnar. "I don't care whether it's the king or a junk dealer from Kisa. I'm not going to wash, that's all."

Aunt Olga, the cook, who was more talkative than Miss Hawk, had said that the man who was coming was a rich grocer, which was certainly far from being a junk dealer. He was bringing his wife along. They didn't have any children of their own to inherit the business one day, and that is why they were coming to Vaesterhaga. To inherit a whole business—that would be something, thought Rasmus. Just imagine having a store filled with all kinds of candy! Of course they probably had things like flour and coffee and soap and herring, too.

"Anyway, I'm going to wash," he said with determination and started to scrub his elbows.

"You just keep on scrubbing," said Gunnar. "I'll help

you." He grabbed Rasmus by the neck and quickly dunked his head in the basin. Rasmus came up, spluttering and furious, while Gunnar stood laughing with his friendly pug-nosed face.

"You aren't mad, I hope," he said teasingly.

Then Rasmus laughed too. He never could stay angry at Gunnar for very long. But he intended to give him a good soaking anyway. He picked up the basin and stalked threateningly toward Gunnar, who stood in front of the dormitory door, awaiting his attack. Rasmus raised the basin. Now Gunnar was really going to get it. But just as he aimed, his target quickly jumped to one side. At the same instant the door opened, and like a violent tropical torrent the contents of the basin splashed over the person standing in the doorway.

That person was Miss Hawk. When such a thing happens, the only one who can keep from laughing is the one who gets drenched. Miss Hawk was far from laughing. But from the boys came muffled giggles, and from Rasmus a shrill, terrified laugh. It lasted for only an instant and then he stood, struck dumb with horror, waiting for the catastrophe. Because there would be one, of that he was sure.

Miss Hawk was a person with a great deal of self-control, which she used now. All she did was shake herself like a wet dog and fix a pair of steely eyes on Rasmus. "I don't have time for you now," she said. "But I'll see you later."

Then she clapped her hands and cried, "You are all to gather in the yard in half an hour. By that time you will have made the beds, cleaned the dormitory, and had breakfast."

Then she left without even glancing at Rasmus. When she had disappeared, bedlam broke out.

"Gosh, what a soaking she got!" said Big Peter. "That time you hit the bull's eye, Rasmus."

But Rasmus couldn't share the general enthusiasm over his aim. This day certainly wasn't beginning very well. It didn't look as if this day were going to mark the turning point in his life, when he would get parents of his own. Punishment was what he was in for, probably terrible punishment, since what he had done was so terrible. He shivered, and his whole body was shaking.

"Get dressed," said Gunnar. "You're so cold you're

turning blue in the face." He added in a subdued voice, "It was all my fault that you threw water on the Hawk."

Still shivering, Rasmus got his shirt and pants on. It didn't make any difference whose fault it was. Neither of them had dreamed that their pranks would have such dreadful consequences. But he was afraid, terribly afraid, of what the Hawk would think up as punishment for him. If any of them did anything really bad, Miss Hawk would beat him with a cane. Big Peter had been thrashed once when he had stolen apples from the parson's garden, and Elof had also got a beating the morning he flew into a rage at Aunt Olga in the kitchen and called her a glutton so that the Hawk heard it. But to pour water over the directress was probably even worse than stealing apples and calling someone a glutton. He was sure that the Hawk would take him to her room and beat him with a cane.

If she beats me, I'll die, thought Rasmus. I'll die on the spot and that's just as well. After all, he was an orphan with straight hair whom no one wanted, and he might as well be dead.

He was as miserable as ever when he came out in the yard where the others were assembled. Miss Hawk was already there, dressed in a neat black dress and a starched white apron. She clapped her hands and said, "As you've probably heard, we're going to have a visit today from a lady and gentleman who will be here in a while to look you over and have a talk with you. You are to behave as usual. It would be preferable of course if you behaved better than usual. Now, start playing!"

Rasmus didn't want to play. He didn't feel as if he would

ever want to play again. Instead he climbed up to his usual perch in the linden tree. There he could be alone to think things out and he could also keep an eye on the road so that he could see the people arriving. Even if he no longer held any hope that they would choose him, it would still be interesting to see what they looked like.

As he sat there under his green arch, waiting, he took the shell and the five-cent-piece out of his pocket and looked at them. It felt good to hold them in his hand. "My treasures," he murmured fondly. "My fine treasures." Despite all his misfortunes, he couldn't help feeling just a little happy about them.

In the distance he heard the faint clatter of horses' hoofs. The sound grew louder and soon a coach was visible at the bend of the road. Two brown horses were trotting along briskly in the dust. When the carriage arrived at the gate, the coachman halted them with a loud "Whoa!"

In the coach were a gentleman and a lady, and oh, how beautiful she was! She was wearing a tiny blue hat with white feathers swaying on her blond hair which was piled up high on the top of her head, and she carried a white lace parasol to protect her from the sun. The parasol was tilted back, so Rasmus was able to see her lovely face. Her cotton dress was also lovely, with its wide, sweeping skirt, and when she got out of the carriage she held it up with her small white hand. Rasmus thought that she looked just like a fairy. The chubby little man who helped her out wasn't at all handsome. He certainly didn't look as if he came out of a fairy tale. But he did have a store filled with candy and licorice sticks, and that made up for a lot.

The lady with the parasol walked with dainty little steps through the gate which her husband held open for her. Rasmus leaned forward as far as he could so that he wouldn't miss the least detail of her fairy-like appearance. How would it feel to have someone like that for a mother?

"Mother," he said to himself, just to hear how it sounded.

Oh, if this would turn out to be his lucky day after all! Then the beautiful lady would know right away that no one, no one in all of Vaesterhaga, would be a better son than he. As soon as she saw him she would say, "That boy with the straight hair is exactly what I'm looking for." Then the grocer would nod and say, "Yes, he might be useful around the store. Perhaps he could be in charge of the candy counter." And when Miss Hawk would come to take him to her room for a beating, the grocer would say, "Please don't touch our boy."

Then they would take him along in the carriage and he would hold the pretty lady's hand. The Hawk would be standing at the gate with her cane, just gaping. As the carriage rolled along the road and the sound of hoofs died away, she would cry a little and say, "There goes Rasmus."

He sighed. If there only weren't so many girls with curls in the world! Greta and Anna-Stina and Elna—three of them in this orphanage alone. Elin, too, but she was queer, so they probably wouldn't want her.

Quickly he scrambled down from the tree. The grocer and his wife were already in the yard and any minute they could pick a curly-haired girl. He would at least show himself before then, and then they could blame themselves if they didn't want him.

With determination he strode toward the yard where Miss Hawk had just welcomed the visitors. "Let's have some coffee in the garden while we're discussing the situation," she said, giving them her biggest smile. "You can be looking the children over in the meantime."

The pretty lady also smiled and looked shyly around the group of children. "Yes, then we can decide. . . ."

Her husband gave her a reassuring pat on the shoulder. "Fine," he said. "Now we'll have some coffee while we talk."

The children were playing ball in the playground close by. They had been told to play and that is what they were doing. But it was a chore and no one was enjoying it. How could they play when their whole future depended on how they conducted themselves and how they happened to look that morning? Many furtive glances were cast in the direction of the three who were sitting at the table by the lilac bush. There was an oppressive silence at the playground. No one quarreled; no one laughed. The only sound that could be heard was the smack of the bat hitting the ball, and it was a strangely painful sound this quiet summer morning.

Like a frightened lamb who has been separated from the flock Rasmus came running from behind the lilac bush. He had no idea that Miss Hawk and her guests were sitting at the garden table, and when he discovered them it was too late to turn back and go another way. He had to pass directly in front of them, and he did so with a pained expression on his face and walking as if his legs were made of wood. He glanced at Miss Hawk out of the corner of his eye. He was close to her, much too close for comfort, and in his hurry to get away and join the rest of the group he stumbled all over the place. He also glanced at the pretty lady, who just at that moment looked at him. He froze to the spot and just stood there, staring, embarrassed.

"Rasmus—" said Miss Hawk sharply, but she stopped short. After all, these people had come to look at the children.

"Oh, is your name Rasmus?" said the pretty lady.

Rasmus was unable to answer. He only nodded.

"How about making a bow when you introduce yourself?"

"Would you like a cookie?" said the lady, taking one from the basket.

Rasmus blushed and made a hasty bow, at the same time looking in Miss Hawk's direction. Was he allowed to take the cookie or not?

Miss Hawk nodded and Rasmus accepted it.

"How about saying 'Thank you' when someone gives you something?" Miss Hawk said.

Rasmus became still redder. He stood there twisting and turning, not knowing what to do. He didn't dare eat the cookie and he didn't know if he was supposed to leave or stay.

"Run along and play now," said Miss Hawk, and Rasmus turned and abruptly ran as fast as his legs could carry him. Miserable, he sat down on the lawn next to the playground and ate his cookie. He had behaved like a fool, standing there so stupidly and not having the sense to bow and say "Thank you." Now the lady must think that he was pretty hopeless.

The sun was almost directly overhead now. It was a clear, beautiful summer day and they didn't have to dig up potatoes. But it was a terrible day of suspense for the children at Vaesterhaga. The ball playing soon came to an end. No one had the courage even to pretend that it was fun. They didn't know how to use this unusual free time which had been given to them and which they knew would last exactly as long as it took those people to make up their minds. Never had a morning seemed so long. They stood around in small, listless groups, watching the lady with the parasol. Her husband remained at the table reading the paper. It was obviously his wife who was going to make the choice. The lady walked from group to group. She talked with them, embarrassed and a little shy. She didn't exactly know what to say to all these poor creatures who were staring at her so pathetically.

There was that little boy Rasmus. He was staring more intently than the rest and there was a pleading look in his eyes, which were dark and seemed much too big for his narrow, freckled face. But there were others whose eyes also had an imploring look. There was that little chubby girl with the red cheeks and a mop of blond, curly hair falling over her forehead. It was impossible to avoid her because she clung like a burr. She was a bold little thing, the only one of the children who dared to smile back.

The lady stroked her cheek and said encouragingly, "What is your name, little girl?"

"Greta," she said and made a pretty curtsy. "What a pretty parasol you have."

The white lace parasol was indeed pretty. The lady gave it

a twirl, but as she did so she happened to drop it on the lawn. Before she could bend down to pick it up Greta was there. But not only Greta. Rasmus had been standing close by, as close to the pretty lady as he could get. He pounced on the parasol. At last he would have a chance to show that he too could be polite.

"Let go," cried Greta, tugging at the parasol.

"No, let me," said Rasmus.

"Let go," cried Greta again, and she gave another tug. Suddenly Rasmus stood there staring dumbfounded at a loose handle in his hand. Greta was holding the rest of the parasol. She was just as horrified. When she finally realized what had happened, she started to cry.

Miss Hawk came running to the scene. "Rasmus, you are impossible," she said. "I think you've gone out of your mind today. Will you ever learn to behave decently?"

Tears of shame and embarrassment came into Rasmus' eyes and he blushed violently.

The lady stood there, unhappy at seeing so much heartbreak. "It's nothing," she said kindly. "The handle can be screwed back on. My husband can fix it."

She took the broken parasol and hurried over to her husband, who was still sitting at the table. Greta quickly dried her tears and trotted behind like a little dog. She stopped a few paces away and watched with interest as the grocer screwed the handle back on the parasol.

"I'm so glad you could fix it," she said, smiling, her blond curls shimmering in the sun.

But Rasmus had disappeared. He had retreated to the bathroom to hide his shame and his unmanly tears. It was

a peaceful place to lick your wounds and the best place to
forget unhappy things. Among the pile of newspapers lying there he could always find something interesting to read,
and for the moment he was able to forget all the grocers'
wives and lace parasols in this whole cruel world.

Rasmus sat there deeply engrossed in his reading. He had
stumbled on something really exciting. Eagerly, he spelled
his way through the article, which read:

ROBBERY AT SANDOE FACTORY
A daring holdup took place yesterday at Sandoe factory.
Two masked bandits forced their way into the office and with

pointed guns escaped with the week's payroll for the entire factory, without leaving any traces.

Rasmus saw those masked men before his eyes and he shivered with excitement. Just now the pretty lady was far from his mind.

But when the visitors left Vaesterhaga a few hours later, he stood at the gate and stared after the carriage, long after it was out of sight. In the back seat was Greta, her blond head next to the blue hat with the feathers, and holding the pretty lady securely by the hand.

3. It's All Over Now

"What did I tell you?" said Gunnar when the carriage had disappeared. "They always pick girls with curly hair."

Rasmus nodded. It was true, all right. Boys didn't have a chance if there were girls with curly hair around.

Still, he refused to give up the hope that somewhere in the world there could be someone who would like to have a boy with straight hair. Someone . . . somewhere . . . far beyond that bend in the road.

"You know what we could do?" said Rasmus eagerly. "We could take off and look for parents ourselves."

"What are you talking about? What parents?" Gunnar didn't follow.

"Parents who would want you. If there was no one else to choose from, they would have to take you, even if you didn't have curly hair."

"Sure, you ought to go up to Miss Hawk and say, 'Please excuse me. I can't dig up potatoes today because I'm going out to look for someone who wants me.' You're crazy."

"Stupid, we'd take off without asking Miss Hawk, of course."

"Well, go ahead and run away," said Gunnar. "You'll probably come back when you're good and hungry, and if you've never had a beating before, you'll get it then."

A beating, Gunnar had said. A shock went through Rasmus. How could he have forgotten the terrible thing that was awaiting him? The Hawk was going to beat him with a cane—he was almost sure of that. The thought made his blood run cold.

"Come on, let's play ball with the others," said Gunnar. "Or are you planning to leave right away?"

Gunnar put his arm around Rasmus' shoulders. He was nice, Gunnar was, and his arm was comforting. Rasmus felt calmer as he walked over to the playground with Gunnar.

The others were standing in a circle around Big Peter, who with an affected smile and mincing walk was imitating the grocer's wife.

"What's your name, my little friend?" he said and patted Elof on the head. "Do you like it at Vaesterhaga? Have you ever seen an automobile? Did you ever wet your pants?"

None of them had heard the grocer's wife say the last part, but they all laughed gleefully. It felt good to be able to make fun of the person who had caused so much secret anguish and so much longing and who would never come back, looking pretty in a blue hat and carrying a lace parasol.

"Here is the boy with the basin," shouted Big Peter when Rasmus and Gunnar approached. "What sort of water tricks are you planning to play on the Hawk tomorrow?"

Rasmus was in no mood to talk about water tricks, but

when Big Peter condescended to talk to you, you had to play along.

"Well, perhaps I can borrow the garden hose and spray her a bit," he said with a superior air.

Everyone laughed and Rasmus, encouraged by his success, continued, "Or else I may use the big fire extinguisher to give her a good soaking."

Oddly enough, no one laughed at this. They all suddenly stood in dead silence staring at something behind Rasmus. With a sinking feeling in his stomach he turned around to see what it was.

It was the Hawk, dressed in her good hat and her black coat with the puff sleeves. She was on her way to a coffee party at the vicarage. Why, oh, *why* did she have to come sneaking up here just at this moment?

"So you're going to give me a soaking, are you?" said Miss Hawk, and there was almost a look of amusement on her face. "Come to my room tomorrow morning at eight o'clock and we'll see who is going to get the soaking."

"Yes, Hawk, Miss—" stammered Rasmus, beside himself with mortification.

Miss Hawk shook her head in despair. " 'Hawk, Miss . . .' I don't know what has gotten into you today, Rasmus."

Then she left and Rasmus stood there, knowing that all was lost. Nothing could save him this time, that was sure. He would be thrashed with a cane and he knew himself that he had deserved it. You couldn't do as much mischief in one day as he had done without being punished.

"Bah, she doesn't hit so hard," said Big Peter consolingly. "It isn't so bad. You don't have to go around looking as if your last hour had come."

But Rasmus had never in his life been beaten with a cane and he was sure he wouldn't be able to stand it. Nothing could make him go through with it. Oh, why wasn't he sitting in the carriage next to the grocer's wife right now, watching Vaesterhaga disappear forever? There was only one thing for him to do—run away. He couldn't lie in bed all night knowing that as soon as it was morning he would have to go to Miss Hawk and be beaten. But he could hardly run away alone. Gunnar had to come along. He just had to! Rasmus was going to talk to him and beg him to come along. There was no time to lose. They would have to leave in a couple of hours.

The long day was over. It was bedtime, but they all delayed going indoors as long as they could. Since the Hawk was away, Aunt Olga was keeping track of the time. But she had no authority. The girls obediently went inside when they were called, but she had to drive the boys ahead of her like a flock of unwilling cattle. No one wanted to go indoors on a beautiful summer evening like this.

Rasmus kept close to Gunnar, and while they were undressing he whispered, "Gunnar, I'm going to run away tonight and you have to come with me!"

Impatiently Gunnar shoved him aside. "Stop talking such nonsense. Why on earth would you do that?"

Rasmus didn't want to admit, even to Gunnar, that it was fear of the cane which drove him away. "I'm through with

this old place," he said. "I'm going to look for another place
to live."

"Well, go, then," said Gunnar, unconcerned. "But I feel
sorry for you when you come back."

"I'll never come back."

The words sounded frightening and Rasmus shuddered
as he said them. He had been at Vaesterhaga ever since he
was a baby. He didn't remember any other home or any
other mother than Miss Hawk. In a way it was awful to
think of leaving for good. It certainly would seem strange
never to see the Hawk again, come to think of it. Not because he liked her, but still . . .

He remembered one night several years ago when he had
an earache, she had taken him in her lap. He had leaned his
sore ear against her arm and she had sung him a lullaby.
He had liked her so much then, and he had liked her for a
long, long time afterward, and almost hoped for another
earache. But he didn't get one and Miss Hawk had never
again paid any attention to him, and hardly ever stroked
him when she made her nightly rounds. And now she was
going to beat him! It would serve her right if he ran away.
But even so, it sounded horrible to say that he was never
coming back.

Then there was Gunnar. If he didn't come along, Rasmus
would probably never see him again, either. That would be
worse than anything else. Gunnar, his best friend! Never to
see him again! They had their beds next to each other in the
dormitory, they sat next to each other in school, and once
behind the chicken coop they had become blood brothers

by pricking their arms and then mixing each other's blood. Now Gunnar didn't want to run away.

Rasmus was hurt and angry. "Are you going to hang around Vaesterhaga until the moss grows on you?"

"We'll talk about that when you come back," said Gunnar.

"I'm never coming back," said Rasmus emphatically, and again the words frightened him as he spoke them.

At first there was bedlam in the dormitory. Big Peter said you could get away with anything when Aunt Olga was in charge. This was a night to have fights and horse around and make noise, and put off going to bed. But then Aunt Olga came in, furious and red as a beet, threatening to tell Miss Hawk. The time had come to get into bed. But they didn't have to quiet down just yet.

"I'm a prince of royal blood," said Albin over in his corner. That was the way he always began. "Prince Albin of the Blood" they called him. He claimed that his father was a member of the royal family and that he, Albin, had landed at Vaesterhaga by mistake.

"All this happened when I was a baby," said Albin. "But when I grow up I'm going to find my father. Then you'll really see something. All of you who have been nice to me will get presents, lots of presents."

"Thank you, Your Majesty," said Big Peter. "Tell us what sort of presents we'll get."

This was a never-ending game. No one but Albin believed he was a prince of the blood and no one but Albin thought that he would ever be in a position to give away so much as a penny. But they all longed for presents which they had never got and never would get, so they listened eagerly to Albin who while lying in bed at night would give away bicycles, books, skates, and games to everyone in sight.

Rasmus had always enjoyed playing this game. But tonight he had only one wish—that they all would fall asleep as quickly as possible. He was all nerves lying there. It was as if all the misfortunes of the day had got under his skin and were working together to drive him away. Outside the open window the summer night was clear and still. Everything was so peaceful and there were no canes threatening. Perhaps, too, somewhere far away, there would be a place for orphans with straight hair that would be better than Vaesterhaga.

He dozed off, but his anxiety awakened him and he felt that the moment had come. There was no sound in the dormitory now, except Elof's snoring, which could be heard over the quiet breathing of the others.

Cautiously Rasmus sat up, his eyes wandering along the rows of beds to make sure that everyone was asleep. Yes, the coast was clear. Prince Albin was mumbling in his sleep and Emil was tossing as usual, but they all slept, including Gunnar. There he lay peacefully with his shaggy head on the pillow, not caring that his best friend was about to disappear forever from Vaesterhaga Orphanage. Rasmus took a deep breath. How sad Gunnar would be when he woke up in the morning and saw that Rasmus really had run away. Gunnar would not have told him so calmly to go ahead if he had believed that Rasmus was serious. He just didn't understand that Rasmus *couldn't* stay there knowing what was in store for him. Again Rasmus sighed deeply. The other boys didn't seem to think that the business with the cane was anything to worry about. Apparently Rasmus was the only one who felt that he would rather die than be beaten.

He crept out of bed as quietly as he could and got dressed without making a sound. His heart was pounding fast and his legs felt stiff and queer. They didn't seem to want to run away, the way they were trembling.

He put his hand in his pants pocket. There were the shell and the coin. Five cents wouldn't get him very far but it would save him once from starving. It would buy him a bun and some milk. But the shell, so beautiful to look at and so smooth to touch, he would leave to Gunnar as a remembrance of his childhood friend, gone forever. When he woke up in the morning there would be no Rasmus next to him, but the beautiful shell would be lying on his bed. Rasmus swallowed hard as he put the shell next to his friend. For a while he stood there, struggling against the tears and listening to Gunnar's deep breathing. Then he put his hand on the pillow and with a chapped, dirty forefinger he gently stroked Gunnar's coarse hair. He wanted to touch his very best friend since this was probably the last time he would ever see him.

"Good-by, Gunnar," he mumbled. Then he tiptoed toward the door. He stopped and listened, his heart pounding loudly. Then he opened the door with a hand which was clammy and shaking, furious at the door because it creaked as if it wanted to give him away.

The steps down to the kitchen also creaked noisily. Just suppose he should meet the Hawk—what would he say then? That he had a stomach ache and had to go to the bathroom? He could never make the Hawk believe that if he met her on the kitchen steps.

He would see if he could find something to eat to take along with him. He tried the pantry door. It was locked. There wasn't even a crust in any of the bread boxes, but he did find one small zwieback, which he put in his pocket.

The kitchen window was open. He would only have to climb up on the table in front of the window and then with one leap he would be free!

But just at that moment he heard steps in the gravel outside, steps which were only too familiar. It was the Hawk coming home from the coffee party at the vicarage.

Rasmus' legs seemed to wilt under him. There was no way out. If the Hawk came in through the kitchen door it was the end. There would be no possible way of explaining his presence in the kitchen at eleven o'clock at night. He listened, stiff with fright. Perhaps there was just the faintest hope that she would go along the veranda.

She didn't. He heard her steps on the kitchen porch. She put her hand on the door knob. Rasmus' paralyzed legs suddenly came to life and he threw himself down under the drop-leaf table. He pulled and tugged at the oilcloth cover to get it to hide as much of him as possible. The next instant Miss Hawk was standing in the kitchen. Rasmus felt as if his last moment had come. It just wasn't possible to be so terrified and still live. He could hardly stand the way his heart was pounding; it was ready to burst.

Every corner of the big, old-fashioned kitchen was lit by the pale glow of the summer night. Miss Hawk would only have to lower her eyes ever so slightly and she would

see Rasmus crouching there under the table like a scared rabbit.

But Miss Hawk seemed to have other things on her mind. She was standing in the middle of the floor, mumbling to herself, "Worries, worries, nothing but worries!"

Although Rasmus was half out of his wits, he couldn't keep from wondering what Miss Hawk meant. What sort of worries could she possibly have? Well, he would never have a chance to find out now. As he watched her standing there, pulling the hatpin out of her hat, it was probably the last time he would ever see her. At least he hoped so.

With a deep sigh Miss Hawk walked out of the kitchen.

The little bang as the door closed behind her was the most wonderful sound Rasmus had ever heard.

He remained crouched under the table for a few tense moments, listening. Then he quickly crawled up on the windowsill and jumped out, landing on the lawn with a thud. The grass was wet from the dew and felt cold under his bare feet. The night air was chilly but it was good to breathe because it was the air of freedom. He was free, thank goodness, he was free!

But he had rejoiced too soon. A new sound again frightened him half out of his wits. The window of Miss Hawk's room on the upper floor was suddenly opened. He heard her unfasten the lock and there she stood, tall and black, staring out toward him. Frantic, he pressed himself against the trunk of an apple tree as if he wanted to disappear into it. He held his breath.

"Is there anyone there?" the Hawk called out.

Rasmus shuddered when he heard the familiar voice. He realized that it was best to answer before she discovered him. It would only make things worse if he kept still. But he couldn't get a word through his trembling lips, and all he could do was stand there and stare up, terror-stricken, toward the dark figure in the window. He was sure that she was looking right at him and he expected her to call his name at any moment.

Oddly enough, she didn't, but abruptly closed the window and disappeared into the room. Rasmus heaved a sigh of relief. He could see her moving about up there. A light was turned on and he saw her shadow against the wall with the blue flowered wallpaper and the photograph of

the royal family. To think that he would never again see that picture or the one with Jesus before Pilate which hung on the opposite wall! That was too bad, because he had enjoyed looking at those pictures when he had been allowed to come into the Hawk's room on some rare occasion. But that was over now. Tomorrow morning at eight o'clock he wouldn't be here, that was sure.

He was very anxious to get away, but he couldn't seem to make himself move as long as he saw the shadow on the wall up there. It was an uncanny feeling to be standing out here watching the Hawk without her knowing it.

Good-by, Hawk, he said to himself. If you had been a little nicer to me when you made your nightly rounds perhaps I would have stayed. But it's all over now.

Perhaps the Hawk could hear his thoughts, because now she was pulling down the shade. It was as if she were saying good-by and were closing Vaesterhaga Orphanage to him and leaving him alone out in the night.

For a moment longer he stood in the shadow of the apple tree looking at his former home. It was an old white house, and tonight it looked so beautiful with its dark windows, surrounded by big trees. To Rasmus, at least, it was beautiful, though Aunt Olga was always saying that it was an awful old barn, impossible to keep clean. But there must be better houses to live in, thought Rasmus, so he didn't have to feel sad about leaving. He would probably find a very good home—there must be other grocers' wives in the world.

He started to run across the wet grass, between the apple trees and down to the gate. Outside the road wound before him like a ribbon. He kept on running farther into the summer night.

4. Paradise Oscar

"I'm not afraid on the open road" was part of a poem the teacher had read to them at school. It was about a boy who also was out alone at night.

Rasmus ought not to be any more afraid than that boy. But still it was awful to be all alone. He wasn't used to it. At the orphanage there were always children around. As a matter of fact, if you wanted to be by yourself there, you had either to go to the bathroom or to climb into the linden tree.

It was a rare treat to be alone at Vaesterhaga. But to be out alone on this chilly, windless night with its pale stars wasn't like anything Rasmus had ever experienced before. The stillness and the weird light, which made everything look so unreal, frightened him. Once, in a dream, he had seen the countryside flooded in a strange light. But he hadn't known that a summer night was like this outside a dream.

Shivering and miserable, he ran along the road as fast as he could, his bare feet slapping against the ground. He was in a hurry because he was afraid of meeting people who might suspect that he had run away. But a little farther along there was a shortcut through the fields which must also lead out into the world. It was a narrow, winding road where only timber carts came through in winter and milk wagons in the summer when the cows were grazing nearby. There he wouldn't have to be afraid of meeting anyone who would wonder what he was doing out alone at that hour of night. But at the fork in the road he hesitated. It looked so ghostly in there among the hazel shrubs, and the poplars were rustling and sighing, although there was no breeze stirring.

"I'm not afraid on the open road. . . ." If only Gunnar had been along! If only he had someone to hold by the hand. The shadows were so deep and the whole world was as quiet as if it were dead. All the birds and animals were asleep, and all people too. Only he was out here alone and afraid—terribly afraid on the open road is what he was and not at all as brave as the little boy in the poem. "It's so far away, deep into the forest," the poem continued, and how true that was!

On top of everything he was so hungry. He pulled the zwieback out of his pocket and ate it, but his stomach still felt just as empty and he wondered anxiously whether there were any kind people in the world who would give a lonely orphan something to eat, even if he did have straight hair and wouldn't be suitable for adoption.

He was getting terribly tired, too. He had to try to find a place where he could sleep. But not just yet. He had to get as far away from Vaesterhaga as possible before dawn —before they discovered that he wasn't in his bed. Just think what commotion that was going to make! Maybe the Hawk would send the police after him.

The very thought made him walk faster. With his hands in his pockets and his shoulders hunched he trudged along the road, staring straight ahead, careful not to look to either side in the dark where the shadows loomed. He walked on and on, feeling terribly abandoned and alone.

The short summer night can be endless if you keep going until your feet refuse to move, your eyelids close, and you stumble along nodding, practically asleep. The dawn comes and the first rays of sun filter through the trees, but you don't see it. Dew drops glitter on the cobwebs and on the leaves of the wildflowers. The light morning mist vanishes into nowhere and in a birch tree close by a thrush, fresh as the morning, raises his voice in jubilation. But you don't notice it. You're so tired you're way beyond caring.

At last Rasmus came to a little gray barn, just the kind that tramps like to sleep in. It was in a field and looked so inviting. At that time of the year such field barns were filled with hay.

With great effort Rasmus pushed open the heavy door. It was dark and still in there, and the hay had such a strong, good smell. With a sigh that was almost a sob he threw himself down and in an instant was fast asleep.

He awoke because he was cold and because a straw was tickling his nose. He flew up with a start, not remembering where he was or how he had got there. But then it all came back to him and a feeling of utter loneliness brought tears to his eyes. He was more miserable than he could have imagined. He was already homesick for Vaesterhaga, Gunnar, his warm bed, and the morning cereal. Now he thought of the orphanage as a lost paradise. Of course there was the

possibility of being thrashed from time to time, but it still wasn't as bad as being all alone in the world and cold and hungry like this.

A small streak of sunlight filtered in through a crack in the wall. His first thought was that since the day was beautiful it would also be less cold. He was wearing his heavy sweater and his gray homespun pants, which Aunt Olga had patched at the knees. But despite that he was so cold that his teeth chattered. He would have preferred to lie down and go back to sleep, but it wasn't possible, cold as he was. Shivering, he sat there in the hay, miserably watching the flecks of dust whirling around in the sunlight.

Then he heard something which sent a cold streak of terror through his whole body from his head to his toes. Someone was *yawning* very close to him! He wasn't alone. Someone else had been sleeping there too. The only parts of him able to move were his eyes, which wandered around trying to discover the source of this horror. Then he saw a curly brown tuft of hair stick up behind a big manger right next to him. He heard a groan and a voice saying, "Ho hum, I'm tired day and night but worst of all in the morning."

Then a head stuck out from behind the manger, showing a round unshaven face with a dark beard. Two eyes stared at him in amazement and then the round face broke into a broad smile. The man didn't look so dangerous and his whole body seemed to chuckle as he said, "Hi there."

"Hi," said Rasmus hesitatingly.

"Golly, you look scared. You think I eat children?"

When Rasmus didn't answer, he continued. "Who are you and what is your name?"

"Rasmus," came the hesitant reply. Rasmus was afraid to answer and afraid not to.

"Rasmus, oh Rasmus," said the bearded man, nodding thoughtfully. "Did you run away from home?"

"No, not—from home," said Rasmus, and he didn't feel as if he were telling a lie. Vaesterhaga wasn't a real home, in any case. How could the man possibly think you'd want to run away from a real home?

"Don't look so terrified," the man said. "I've told you I don't eat children."

Rasmus plucked up his courage.

"Did *you* run away from home?" he asked cautiously.

The bearded man roared with laughter. "Have I run away from home? Yes, that's probably it," he said and laughed still harder.

"Are you a tramp?" asked Rasmus.

"Call me Oscar," the man said as he raised himself in the hay. And Rasmus saw that he must be a tramp because he was wearing such scruffy clothes—a checkered, raggy jacket and trousers which had no shape at all. He was big and burly and kind-looking, and when he laughed his white teeth gleamed in his dark-bearded face.

"Tramp is right. . . . Haven't you ever heard of Paradise Oscar? That's me. The paradise tramp and God's best friend, that's me."

God's best friend! Rasmus began to wonder if that tramp was all right in the head. "Why are you God's best friend?" asked Rasmus.

Many deep wrinkles appeared on Oscar's forehead. "Someone has to be, and what's more there has to be a tramp who is God's best friend. God approves of tramps."

"Does he?" said Rasmus suspiciously.

"Yes he does," Oscar assured him. "When he has gone to so much trouble to put the world together he wants to have everything in it. Don't you understand? How would it look if there was everything except tramps?"

Oscar nodded, apparently pleased with his explanation. "God's best friend, yes sir, that's me."

Then he pulled out a big package wrapped in newspaper from a rucksack lying next to him in the hay.

"A little breakfast is going to hit the spot."

As he said it Rasmus felt as if his stomach were about to

tie itself into knots from hunger. He was so hungry he was ready to start chewing on the hay like a cow.

"I have a bottle of milk standing outside here somewhere," said Oscar.

In one leap he was at the door. It squeaked and moved heavily on its hinges as he pushed it open. A broad carpet of sunshine flowed into the barn. Oscar stood still for a moment, stretching himself in the sun, but then he disappeared. He was back in a second with a well-corked wine bottle full of milk.

"Yes sir, a little breakfast is going to taste mighty good," he said, making himself comfortable in the hay. He unwrapped the newspaper and pulled out big, thick sandwiches made of rye bread. With a contented grunt he sank his teeth into one. Rasmus saw that it had ham in it, his favorite kind of sandwich.

Oscar also seemed to like ham. He would take a bite, look hungrily at the sandwich, and take another bite. Rasmus turned white with hunger. He tried to look in another direction, but it was impossible. The sandwich drew his eyes like a magnet and he felt his mouth begin to water.

Oscar stopped chewing. He put his head to one side and looked teasingly at Rasmus. "I don't suppose you would like a plain ham sandwich?" he said. "Your kind probably eat cereal with raisins for breakfast. An ordinary ham sandwich probably wouldn't appeal to you?"

Do you say no when the splendors of heaven are offered?

"Yes, thank you," said Rasmus and swallowed hard. "Yes, thank you, please."

Without a word Oscar handed him a sandwich. It was wonderfully thick and long and there were two big slices of ham in it. Rasmus took a bite and, oh, the taste of the ham blending with the rich, coarse rye bread! He closed his eyes and ate.

"Milk," said Oscar, and Rasmus opened his eyes again. Oscar handed him a tin mug filled to the brim and he drank in deep drafts. It made his stomach cold and he was even colder than before, but that made no difference. He kept on drinking just the same until there wasn't a single drop left.

"More sandwich?" said Oscar and without a word shoved another torpedo-sized one in his direction.

"May I . . . can you spare it?"

"Yes, go ahead," said Oscar. "Not all farmers' wives are stingy. The one who gave me these must have had a feeling that I would meet up with you."

They sat there quietly in the hay, eating away until there wasn't a crumb left. They finished the milk and Rasmus felt his stomach getting still colder.

"Thank you very much," he said shivering. "That was the best meal I've ever eaten."

"But you're blue in the face," said Oscar. "You'll have to get out in the sun and warm up."

Oscar got up and put on his rucksack and started to walk toward the door. Rasmus saw his big, broad frame in the opening and he realized that Oscar was about to leave. The thought was unbearable. Oscar couldn't leave him alone.

"Oscar," he said in such panic that he could hardly get

the words out. "Oscar, I would like to be a paradise tramp like you."

Oscar turned around and looked at him. "Boys like you shouldn't become tramps. You should stay at home with your father and mother."

"I don't have a father and mother," said Rasmus. Oh, if Oscar would only understand how alone he was and take pity on him! He leaped out of the hay and caught up with Oscar.

"I don't have parents," he said, "but I'm looking for some." He eagerly took Oscar's hand. "Can't you let me go on the road with you while I'm looking?"

"What is it you're looking for?" Oscar asked.

"For someone who wants me," said Rasmus. "Don't you think there might be *someone* who would like a boy with straight hair?"

Flabbergasted, Oscar looked into the thin, freckled face that was so anxiously turned up toward him.

"Yes, sure," he said, "there are people who would like a boy with straight hair. The important thing is that he is honest."

"I'm honest," Rasmus assured him. "That is, more or less," he added. Perhaps it wasn't completely honest to run away from an orphanage.

Oscar gave him a severe look. "Please be good enough to tell me where you come from."

Rasmus lowered his eyes and drilled his big toe into the ground, looking very unhappy. "From Vaesterhaga—from the orphanage. But I won't go back there," he said emphatically, having already forgotten that a while ago he had been longing terribly to get back there. The only thing he was sure of was that he wanted to be with Oscar, whom he had known for hardly an hour.

"Why did you run away?" asked Oscar. "Did you do something bad?"

"Yes," he said, nodding slowly. "I poured water on Miss Hawk."

Oscar laughed, but checked himself. "So you're the mischievous kind, eh? But you haven't stolen anything, I hope?"

"Yes," said Rasmus, covered with guilt and shame.

"Then I can't have you as a pal," said Oscar. "If you steal when you're a tramp, then you're finished. The sheriff will get you before you have a chance to blow your nose. No sir, I can't have you as a partner."

Rasmus clung to him in panic. "Please, please, Oscar," he begged.

" 'Please' doesn't do any good," said Oscar. "What did you steal?"

Rasmus frantically dug in the ground with his big toe again. "A zwieback," he said quietly. "When I was going to run away . . . to have something to eat."

"A zwieback?" Oscar laughed so heartily that his white teeth flashed. "That doesn't count."

Rasmus was tremendously relieved. "Could I get to be one of those God's best friends anyway?"

"Yes, they're not that fussy up there," Oscar assured him.

"Will you let me be your partner, then?"

"Hm," said Oscar. "You can come along for a while and we'll see how we get along together."

"Thank you very much, Oscar," said Rasmus. "I already get along together."

Then they started walking. The sun was still low in the sky, but the village was slowly beginning to come to life. In the distance they heard a rooster crowing, dogs were barking, and on the road an empty haycart rattled by, drawn by two skinny horses. A sleepy farmhand stood upright in the cart holding the reins.

"Let's ask if we can ride with him," suggested Rasmus.

"You'll do no such thing. You have to lie low for a while. You never know. Miss Hawk may be so crazy about you that she'll ask the sheriff to find you and bring you back."

"Do you think she'd do that?" said Rasmus, shivering with both cold and fear.

"I guess she'll wait a couple of days first. She'll probably be thinking that you'll turn up when you're hungry."

"But I won't," said Rasmus, desperately trying to stifle a yawn. "I didn't sleep much last night," he said by way of apology.

He was still desperately tired and sleepy, but he didn't want to be any trouble to Oscar, who was tramping along in such a free and easy manner and taking such long steps.

"So you would like to hit the sack?" Oscar glanced at the poor, exhausted, frozen boy who was half running beside him to keep up.

"Come on, we'll find a place where you can get warm and where you can sleep."

"I can't sleep in the middle of the day," said Rasmus, astonished. "I've only just got up."

"Tramps can sleep any time," Oscar assured him.

Then it dawned on Rasmus what it meant to be a tramp. In an instant, the wonderful aspects of this new life were revealed to him. You could do exactly what you pleased. You could eat and sleep and go exactly where you pleased. You were free, wonderfully free, like a bird in the forest.

Completely dazzled by his discovery, he trudged along at Oscar's side. He already felt like a tramp and looked at his surroundings with the eyes of a tramp. He looked at the road, winding softly through the landscape ahead of them and seeming to hold exciting things in store behind every bend. The cows were contentedly chewing their cuds in the lush green fields, and outside the farmers' red cottages dairy maids were washing milk bottles and the farmhands were pumping water into troughs for the horses. In the houses children were crying and outside chained dogs were barking and straining at their leashes. In the dairies lonely calves were mooing for the freedom of the fields. Rasmus saw and heard it all through the eyes and ears of a tramp.

Oscar was walking along, singing happily to himself. Suddenly he turned off the road and stopped in a sunny clearing behind some high juniper bushes.

"You can sleep here for a while," said Oscar. "There's shelter and sun here and no one can see you from the road."

Rasmus began to yawn but a terrible thought made him stop with his mouth wide open. "Oscar, you promise not to go away while I'm asleep?"

Oscar nodded. "Just you go ahead and sleep," he said.

Rasmus threw himself down on his stomach and bur-
rowed his nose into the fold of his sleeve. The sun warmed
him so wonderfully and he was so sleepy. As he was sinking deeper and deeper, he felt Oscar spreading his jacket
over him. Now he wasn't cold any longer.

He was lying on a floor of thyme, breathing in the good,
spicy smell. The warmth of the sun also brought out the
fragrance of the juniper bushes. These were summer smells
and all his life they would bring back to him this summer
day on the road.

A bee came buzzing over his head. With an effort he
opened one eye to look at it and he saw Oscar sitting there,
chewing on a blade of grass.

Then he fell into a deep sleep.

5. A Day on the Road

"Please lady, could you spare some food for me and my partner?" Oscar was standing at the kitchen door bowing politely, his cap in his hand.

"Are you on the road again, Paradise Oscar?" said the farmer's wife disapprovingly. "It isn't so long ago that I gave you a whole meat loaf."

"So you did," said Oscar. "But I was lucky enough to live through it."

Rasmus grinned and the farmer's wife gave him a dark look. "Who is that youngster you are dragging around?"

"Oh, it's a poor heathen I've picked up," said Oscar with mock seriousness. "We are looking for a civilized home for him. You don't happen to need a handy little heathen around the house?"

"Heathen yourself." The farmer's wife furiously swished the dishrag over the kitchen table, sweeping crusts of bread, potato peels, and spilled milk onto the floor. She was making it very plain that she disliked tramps and Rasmus almost wished that they would leave again. But this was the first farm kitchen he had been in and he had to use the chance to look around. It certainly didn't smell as good as the kitchen at Vaesterhaga. Here there was a smell from the garbage pails over by the sink which were destined for the pigs, and sour rags and a strange undefinable house smell that he had never met before. He was lucky that they didn't want him on this farm, because he wouldn't have wanted to stay here. They had children enough without him —a whole raft of fat, pasty-faced ones who stood gaping at him, probably because Oscar had said he was a heathen.

"If you chop some wood for me I'll give you something to eat later," said the woman grouchily.

Oscar put his head to one side and looked pleadingly at her. "Do I *have* to chop wood? Can't I play you a little tune instead?"

"Thanks, I can get along without that," the woman growled, but she no longer looked quite so forbidding.

"That's life," Oscar said nodding sadly. "Chopping wood —me! Just goes to show what you can get yourself into while peacefully walking along the road minding your own business."

"Get out to the woodshed and no nonsense," said the woman. But she no longer looked so grouchy.

Oscar and Rasmus moved quickly toward the door. "How are we supposed to know where the woodshed is?" Rasmus asked.

"Hah, I could find it in the dark if I had to," said Oscar. "When I get even close to a woodshed my legs start protesting, and then I say to myself, 'There it is.' And you can bet I'm right."

He went into the shed, which was indeed the woodshed, picked up the ax that lay on the chopping block, and began chopping. Quickly and efficiently he split the big chunks of cord wood. Rasmus picked up the logs and piled them into the cart which was obviously used to fetch wood.

"My, you're good at chopping wood," said Rasmus. "But you're awfully lazy, aren't you?"

Oscar nodded. "Yes, as far as work goes, I can get along on very little."

"Didn't anyone ever offer you a job?"

"Yes, it has happened. But on the whole people are usually nice to me," said Oscar, and he continued philosophically: "It's like this, you see. *Sometimes* I want to work and then I want to work very hard, but sometimes I don't want to work at all. People seem to think you have to work all the time, and that I can't get into my poor head."

"I couldn't get that into my poor head either when I was at Vaesterhaga," Rasmus admitted.

Now the cart was full and Oscar stopped chopping. From his rucksack, which was standing nearby, he pulled out a small accordion carefully wrapped up in a piece of red blanket.

"Now we're going to play a little tune and the old woman can do what she likes." He let his fingers roam over the keys and the notes came out like deep sighs. But then he really got into the spirit and the woodshed was filled with the most wonderful music that Rasmus had heard in all his life.

> "Her hair is as black as the darkest night—
> Is it so strange that she's on my mind?"

sang Oscar in a big, warm voice which made Rasmus tingle with pleasure. This was much better than listening to Miss Hawk playing from *Zion's Songs* on the organ at home. Rasmus made himself comfortable on the chopping block and thoroughly enjoyed himself.

The pasty-faced children stood at a distance, quietly listening. The farmer's wife had made herself an excuse for going to the rhubarb patch right next to where Oscar was. She was energetically breaking off rhubarb stalks and pretending that she neither saw nor heard Oscar. But when he stopped singing, she came up and said in an almost friendly way, "You can go in and eat now."

"Fried herring and potatoes, just like mother used to make," said Oscar, and he slapped his knees in happy anticipation. Rasmus felt the same way. He hadn't eaten a home-cooked meal since he left Vaesterhaga, and the smell of herring and onions made his mouth water. The woman generously put before him five big potatoes and almost a whole herring, and he was beginning to like her. But while he was eating she eyed him curiously, and at last she said, "You know, Oscar, that boy is too small to be wandering around on the roads!"

Oscar had his mouth so full that he almost couldn't talk. "Sure, I know," he said. "But it isn't for long. I was only joking before. The boy is on his way to his father and mother."

That was true, thought Rasmus. As soon as he found someone who wanted him, he wouldn't be a tramp any more. But there was no hurry to find a father and mother now. He wanted to look around first and it was wonderful to be on the road with Oscar. He most certainly didn't want to part from him yet. But maybe Oscar felt that it was a nuisance to have him along? Perhaps he was anxious to find parents for him as soon as possible?

When they started walking again, he asked about it. "Do you want to get rid of me, Oscar?"

Oscar had already fallen into his marching step. "When I want to get rid of you, I'll tell you," he said.

This answer wasn't so very reassuring. Suppose that Oscar told him before he found a new home! What in the world would he do then? He had been alone for a night on the road and that was something he didn't want to repeat ever again. He looked timidly at Oscar. He would be so good and so careful not to cause any trouble if only Oscar wouldn't get tired of him.

"Oscar, I can carry my sweater myself," he said eagerly.

But Oscar didn't think that was a very good idea. "What would be the sense in that when I can put it in the rucksack? The weight makes no difference."

Oscar walked along at his regular pace and Rasmus took as big steps as he could so as not to fall behind. "Do you want me to hold your hand, Oscar?" he asked out of breath when he could no longer keep up.

Oscar stopped and gave him a long look. "Yes, thank you," he said. "Please do. Hold my hand like a good boy so that I won't fall behind."

Rasmus put his hand in Oscar's and they continued at a slower pace.

"I'm not used to this yet," Rasmus mumbled apologetically. He realized that Oscar had slowed down for his sake.

"No, of course you don't become an expert vagabond overnight," Oscar admitted. Then he showed Rasmus how to walk in a steady, even trot. "But we don't have to rush as if we had to get to the end of the world before nightfall," said Oscar. "If we get there tomorrow, it's soon enough."

Rasmus trudged along, overflowing with gratitude because Oscar was so nice. He felt that he wanted to pay him back in some way—make a really big sacrifice for Oscar's sake or give him something so that he would understand how much Rasmus liked him without his having to say it.

They passed one of those little country stores where you could buy everything from rakes, boots, and kerosene to coffee and candy. But, alas, it was a paradise open only to those who had money. Longingly, Rasmus looked in through the open door and his feet seemed to stop by themselves. It would have been so wonderful to stay awhile and look around. But Oscar wasn't going to do any window shopping. He was already well ahead. With a sigh Rasmus hurried to catch up with him. Then he happened to put his hand in his pocket and there was the five-cent piece! He had forgotten all about it during the exciting happenings of the last twenty-four hours. He was overjoyed when he felt the coin between his fingers. What a marvelous thing a five-cent piece was!

"Oscar, do you like butterscotch?" he asked in a voice trembling with excitement.

"Of course I like butterscotch," said Oscar. "Everybody likes butterscotch. But I have no money right now, you see, so we can't buy any."

"Yes, I can," said Rasmus, producing the coin. He was a little worried that Oscar would give him a lecture on thrift, but that worry proved unnecessary.

"Well, isn't that dandy?" said Oscar. "Run over and buy some butterscotch with it then."

Rasmus turned around and ran back. What wonderful luck that he happened to remember the money right here at the store, and he was luckier still that he hadn't spent it before now.

He came back triumphantly to Oscar, who was sitting at the edge of the road waiting for him. It was a moment of indescribable delight to be able to open the bag and show Oscar five big pieces of butterscotch.

Oscar put his head to one side and looked very hungry. "Now, let's see which one I want."

"You have to take all of them," Rasmus cried eagerly. "I want you to take all of them!"

But Oscar waved this generosity aside with his hand. "No, moderation in everything. One of those is enough for me."

That Oscar happened to be such a moderate butterscotch eater made him still more perfect in Rasmus' eyes. With all his heart he had wanted to give Oscar all five pieces, but he wasn't more than human, and besides, he was awfully fond of butterscotch.

To be sitting there on the roadside taking the paper off the deliciously sticky candy was certainly one of the nicest ways of spending time that Rasmus could think of. You finally had to put the whole thing in your mouth to get the paper off. Then it came off easily and there was only the chewy, wonderful butterscotch left. If you sucked it sparingly it could last a long, long time.

"Like this," said Rasmus as he demonstrated the technique of slow sucking to Oscar. If Oscar had taught him how to walk he would show Oscar how to eat butterscotch.

For a long time they sat in the sunshine, sucking away, but no matter how economical they were, the butterscotch slowly but surely shrank until finally all that was left was a syrupy taste in the mouth.

"Let's save the others," suggested Oscar. "If we ever get into a tight spot it might be nice to have a little butterscotch in reserve." Little did he realize how right he was.

When it began to get dark they stopped by a small lake. It had been a warm day and they had come a long way. Rasmus was exhausted, and at first all he wanted to do was to stretch out on a rock, but the longing for a swim got the better of him. He quickly stripped behind a bush.

Oscar took a small mirror, some soap, and a razor out of his rucksack and began to lather his face. "Don't go out too far," he said. "The water nymph might come and take you."

"Oh pooh, I can swim," said Rasmus, and with a little pang of regret he remembered how Gunnar and he had learned to swim in the river at home. It seemed at least a thousand years ago.

The water felt smooth and warm on his body, and it was so pleasant to swim around in it. All his tiredness seemed to vanish. The water lilies swayed as he swam by them. They had a lovely phosphorescent sheen to them. Was this perhaps the water nymph's own garden where she picked water lilies on summer nights?

Rasmus turned on his back and lay floating for a while, contemplating his big toes, which stuck up out of the water. Along the shore everything was still. On the other side of the lake a cuckoo was warbling such a melancholy chant that it somehow made Rasmus feel melancholy too.

"That cuckoo is crazy," said Oscar. "Midsummer has come and gone and he is supposed to turn into a hawk. Doesn't he know that?"

"The teacher at school told us that it's only an old wives' tale that the cuckoo turns into a hawk after midsummer," Rasmus called out from the water.

"Prove it," said Oscar.

"Prove! You are supposed to be God's best friend so you shouldn't need much proof."

"No, you're right there." Oscar had finished shaving, and now he got out a brass comb and started to work on his curly hair. "You're awfully smart to be so little."

In a neighboring field some cows were grazing. They came up to the fence and stood and stared at the trespassers. One of the cows lumbered heavily down to the water to drink and from her bell came a clear little tinkle.

Summer sounds, thought Rasmus. As he lay there in the water the only sounds he could hear were the tinkling of that bell, the cuckoo over on the other side of the lake, and the little splashings of his own movements in the water.

Oscar was also aware of these summer sounds, because

as he sat there trying to untangle his hair, he absent-mindedly started to sing:

"Now we have summer,
Now we have sun,
Now we have buttercups in the meadows. . . ."

Then he stopped singing and looked at himself in the mirror with a disgusted expression. His hair was just as unruly as before; with a shrug he put the comb back in the rucksack.

"Aren't you coming for a swim?" Rasmus called out to him.

"No, but I'm going to wash my feet." Oscar pushed his trouser legs up and ventured cautiously into the water. "I've already had a bath," he said.

"When?"

"Last year, in honor of our royal family," said Oscar. "It was May fifteenth, the queen's name day, and cold as the dickens. I don't want to do that over again. It's just as easy to keep clean bit by bit."

"How are you going to prove that?" said Rasmus.

"Like this," said Oscar. But just then he slipped and fell. He sat in the water up to his waist, looking stunned. Rasmus shouted with laughter and Oscar glowered at him.

"As I started to say—I'll show you," he growled when he had managed to get up on his feet again. But he was no longer in a bad humor. Sitting on a rock, he carefully washed his feet and then waded back to the shore in his wet pants, singing a snatch of a song to himself about summer and sun and swimming in the sea.

"Oscar, I like you," Rasmus shouted after him, and he didn't know himself what made him do it just then.

It was time to have supper. Oscar had made a fire between the rocks to dry his pants and to keep away the mosquitoes—"and to be like Indians," added Rasmus, creeping as close to the fire as he could.

During the afternoon they had stopped at a big estate and been given milk and sandwiches to take with them, because Oscar had sung and played for all he was worth—songs about "Ida's Grave" and "The Lion's Bride" and a lot of others that Rasmus had never heard before.

Now, as he was taking the sandwiches out of their newspaper wrapping, he noticed that there was a story about those robbers in this paper too. "No sign of the Sandoe robbers," it said. "The police are combing the area." Rasmus showed Oscar the article. "Where is Sandoe?" he asked.

"It's about three or four miles from here," said Oscar.

Rasmus spread out the sandwiches on the rock. "The ones with the cheese are Lion's Bride sandwiches, and the ones with the sausage are Ida's Grave sandwiches," he said.

"And this is the Avesta waterfall," said Oscar as he tilted the bottle of milk into his mouth.

Rasmus hungrily wolfed a sausage sandwich. "She was so nice and pretty, the lady of that house," he said dreamily. "But she already had two girls with curls."

"Otherwise she could have had you?"

"Yes," said Rasmus, and his eyes sparkled in the glow from the fire. "Yes, that's it. I would like to live with someone who is pretty and rich."

"Ho hum," said Oscar.

Mosquitoes were buzzing around them and as the fire
died down they became bolder.

"Now we're going to fool those bloodsuckers by hitting
the hay," said Oscar. He got some lake water in his mug,
threw it on the embers, and packed his belongings together.

There was a farmhouse close by. Oscar had been there

before and asked for permission to sleep in the hayloft.
Rasmus made himself comfortable and covered himself with
hay so that only his nose stuck out. He wanted to give the
mosquitoes as little of himself as possible.

"Are you all right?" Oscar asked when he too had got
settled.

"Yes, except for my hind legs. They feel a little weak,"
said Rasmus.

"Sleep will take care of that," said Oscar, and he yawned.

Rasmus lay awake listening to the rustling and snapping
in the hay. He would have been frightened if Oscar hadn't
been so close. From the barn below he heard the gentle rat-
tling of chains. One of the animals was restless down there.
Over him the mosquitoes buzzed stubbornly. That was the
last thing he heard before he fell into a deep sleep.

6. Hard Times

He awoke with a start a few hours later. A harsh voice was saying, "There he is."

Two policemen were standing only a few feet away from him and he saw Oscar sit up in the hay, wide awake. But he didn't see anything more, because Oscar quickly threw a handful of hay over him.

His heart began to pound and he had a sinking feeling in his stomach. Now the sheriff is going to get me and I'll have to go back to the Hawk, was his first thought.

"What is this all about?" he heard Oscar ask indignantly.

"We'll tell you later," said one of the policemen. "You have to come with us."

Now Oscar was really getting furious. "I'll do no such thing. Here I lie sleeping, innocent as a bride, and you come barging in here waking me up at the crack of dawn. Watch out or I'll really lose my temper."

He slowly rolled around in the hay to get on his feet, and as he did so he whispered to Rasmus, "Lie still! Don't move!"

Then the police left, taking Oscar with them. They were taking Oscar from him—nothing could be worse than that. They just disappeared with him and Rasmus didn't even know where. They had also taken Oscar's rucksack. Rasmus looked through the crack in the door and saw Oscar climb into a cart. One of the policemen sat down next to him and took the reins. The other one sat in the back seat. The farmer and a farmhand stood there gaping, and the wife and the maids stuck their heads out of the kitchen window so as not to miss any of Oscar's humiliating departure. The policeman said "Giddiap" to the horse and away they went. The sound of the horse's hoofs clattering off was a terrible sound to Rasmus. Now he would probably never see Oscar again. Heartbroken, he threw himself down in the hay and tried to stifle his sobs.

Then he heard someone open the barn door. Milk cans were being banged around and some cows were mooing as if the barn were on fire while the two dairy maids were chattering excitedly. Cautiously, he crawled up to the feed hatch to listen. Maybe they were saying something about Oscar.

"You never know what a tramp is up to," he heard one of the girls say. "It wouldn't surprise me if this one is the Sandoe robber."

"That's why they came and got him for questioning," said the other one.

"If he did it, he will go to jail for sure," said the first one with obvious satisfaction.

"If he did it," Rasmus repeated under his breath from his hiding place. Stupid milkmaids, how could they ever get such an idea about God's best friend?

He couldn't bear to stay up here in the hayloft. He just had to find out where Oscar was. If he could only find out where the sheriff lived, he would be able to talk to Oscar somehow. It would be like sticking his head into a lion's den. The sheriff might grab him too and send him back to the orphanage. But if Oscar went to jail it wouldn't matter what happened to him.

Slowly he opened the hayloft door and made sure that there was no one around. Then he quickly ran down the ramp and along the road in the direction in which the cart had disappeared. He ran as long as he was able to. Then he tried to grind along in one of those trots that Oscar had taught him. He had no idea how far it was to the sheriff's office. He hoped to meet someone he could ask, but there were no people on the road this early.

At last an old woman came out of the woods. It was just like the stories in books, Rasmus thought. An old woman always turned up when someone needed to ask the way to the dragon's castle or something like that.

This woman was carrying a bundle of wood on her back and walked stooping forward. She didn't notice Rasmus until she was almost on top of him. Then she raised her head and he saw her tired old eyes under her shawl.

"I would like to know where the sheriff lives," stammered Rasmus.

The old woman at once got a suspicious look in her eyes. "I have permission to gather wood in the forest," she said, and raised a gnarled, crippled finger at him. "I *have* permission from the sheriff." Then she hurried away, turning her head and muttering, "I have permission!"

Discouraged, Rasmus kept on walking. The women in the fairy tales didn't answer that way.

It wasn't long before a milk cart caught up with him. The driver was a boy not much older than Rasmus. He reined in the horse and asked in a friendly way, "Do you want a ride?"

Gratefully, Rasmus climbed into the seat beside the boy. It was a great relief not to have to walk, and besides, he might be able to find out what he wanted to know.

"The sheriff lives in the village over there," the boy told him. "That's where I'm going with the milk. I'll show you because we're going by the lock-up and he lives right behind it in a yellow house."

Evidently the sheriff was still in his yellow house, because when the milk cart rattled past the lock-up, Oscar was sitting on a bench outside, well guarded by the same policemen who had arrested him. Rasmus didn't dare try to attract his attention. Instead he rode as far as the dairy. There he gave the boy one of his pieces of butterscotch as a token of appreciation for the ride, then quickly slipped back along the same narrow street by which they had come.

Oscar was no longer sitting on the bench, but from the sheriff's office Rasmus heard the sound of voices. He crept as close to the open window as he dared and there, luckily enough, was a privet hedge to hide behind.

"Do you think I look like 'two masked men,' eh?" he heard Oscar bellowing. "Tramps have to take the blame for everything in these parts."

"Take it easy, now, Oscar," said a voice which sounded as if it might belong to the sheriff. "We would only like to know what you were doing last Thursday."

"Last Thursday . . . I was eating pork and peas," said Oscar.

"Was that all?" asked the sheriff.

"Yes, and I didn't get any pancake for dessert," he added.

"I mean, is that *all* you did on that day?" the sheriff continued patiently.

"Now how do you expect me to remember that? A tramp only remembers what he eats. I don't keep track of the days. But I distinctly remember that I didn't disguise myself as two masked men in order to steal money."

"We'll have to accept that, then," said the sheriff's voice. "But do you know if any colleagues of yours are around in this area just now?"

"Colleagues—what does that mean? Are they robbers?" asked Oscar.

"No. Tramps, I mean."

"I'll be darned. Are we called colleagues in official language? Here I've lived a whole lifetime thinking I was just an ordinary tramp, and then I turn out to be a colleague."

The sheriff interrupted him. "Have you seen any other tramps in this area lately?"

There was a moment's silence, and then Oscar said, "I've met the Beetle Killer and Seven Up and the Gnome. But if any of them are robbers my name isn't Paradise Oscar."

The sheriff blew his nose and came to stand with his back against the window. "Oh, well," he said, and blew his nose again. "I guess we'll have to let Paradise Oscar go then."

"Yes, being innocent is an extenuating circumstance," said Oscar sarcastically.

The sheriff didn't say anything.

A short while later Oscar came out with his rucksack on his back and started walking down the street. Rasmus ran after him, and when Oscar had turned the corner and was out of sight of the sheriff Rasmus stuck his hand in Oscar's and said, "Are you surprised to see me?"

Oscar grinned. "My old pal. I thought you were going to take off on your own when I got thrown in the jug."

"Oh no, I'm not that kind of a friend. I knew that you would soon get out again because you didn't do it."

"You couldn't know that for sure. It was the Sandoe hold-up they wanted to pin on me, and that happened last Thursday. We didn't even know each other then."

"No, but I know you now," said Rasmus gravely. "So now I know you didn't do it."

"If only sheriffs were that smart!" said Oscar, putting his arm around Rasmus' shoulders. "But sheriffs think that all vagabonds are thieves, worse luck."

They sat down on a bench in a park and each ate an "Ida's Grave" sandwich—the last ones left.

"Now we'll have to sing and play for all we're worth, otherwise we'll starve to death," said Oscar. "One thing I did get out of those cops. No one seems to be looking for a runaway orphan around here yet. But maybe the Hawk isn't such a fast worker."

"Sometimes she's so quick, you have no idea," Rasmus assured him. He got out the bag of butterscotch from his pocket. "Now we've had hard times," he said. "I think we ought to finish the butterscotch."

They ate the two pieces which were left and then Oscar said, "It was nice of the sheriff to give me a ride because I was coming here anyway. I usually play at the houses around here. These people are less stingy than farmers. Farmers only give me food."

"That's not so bad either," said Rasmus, who was starving, in spite of the sandwich and the butterscotch.

Oscar got up from the bench. "But I like to be paid in cash. That reminds me. I think we'll go and say hello to old Mrs. Hedberg."

"Who is Mrs. Hedberg?"

"She's the world's nicest little old lady. She has lots of money and parts with it easily. I sometimes sing 'Every Forest Has Its Spring' for her and then she cries and gives me fifty cents."

Rasmus leaped with delight. " 'Every Forest Has Its Spring'—I know that too. Aunt Olga in the kitchen used to sing it."

"Aunt Olga in the kitchen had the right idea, it seems to me. Well then we can go and crow for old Mrs. Hedberg, both of us."

Rasmus skipped gaily along the sidewalk. What fun to be singing with Oscar! And to be able to earn money for it, too! He gave his pal a fond look. "It would probably be a good thing, Oscar, if I learned all your songs in case you should get hoarse some day."

Oscar nodded. "If I should get hoarse it would be just fine if you could take over 'The Lion's Bride' and 'Ida's Grave.' "

Mrs. Hedberg's house was way over at the other end of town. It was an old green villa shaded by huge maple trees, at a considerable distance from its neighbors.

Rasmus and Oscar hesitated politely at the gate. It wasn't proper for wandering minstrels to come up to the house too abruptly. They had to approach slowly and diffidently.

The fragrance of the jasmine was overpowering and the bleeding heart was in its loveliest pale red bloom. Mignonette and gilly-flowers grew in the borders but there were also pigweed, "dirty dick," chickweed, and other weeds of that kind.

"The Hawk would go out of her mind if she saw a garden like this one," said Rasmus.

"Mrs. Hedberg is so old," said Oscar by way of explanation. "She can't keep the place going any more and her maid is too lazy, I suppose."

They walked up the garden path to the house. There was an absolute stillness over the whole place and the shades were drawn. It looked so deserted you wouldn't think anyone lived there.

"I hope that little old Mrs. Hedberg isn't dead," said Oscar. The merry chirping of the sparrows on the veranda was the only sound that broke the silence. "We have to put some life into this place," he said and pulled out his accordion. "Let's go."

Rasmus cleared his throat. This was the first time he had ever sung in public.

"Every forest has its spring
And flowers in the fields. . . ."

Rasmus thought they sang wonderfully together, Oscar and he.

"And every heart its story . . ."

They didn't get any farther, because just then a shade was pulled up and Mrs. Hedberg's maid stuck her head out of the window. At least Rasmus assumed that it was Mrs. Hedberg's maid, because she was dressed in one of those blue uniforms with a white apron which maids in fine houses used to wear.

"You can't sing here," she said. "The lady of the house is sick and doesn't want to be disturbed. Be on your way!"

Oscar doffed his hat. "Please convey my humble greetings to Mrs. Hedberg. Tell her that Paradise Oscar wishes her a speedy recovery."

The maid didn't answer. She just pulled down the shade again.

"That one certainly is a shrew," said Oscar. "The old lady used to have a nice maid who asked me in for coffee. I wonder where she is?"

Rasmus was terribly disappointed. He had been hoping that Mrs. Hedberg might even give them as much as fifty cents. Even Oscar was disappointed. "Life can't always be a bowl of cherries," he said and started to walk toward the gate. "Come, let's go."

But Rasmus stopped him. "Oscar, I'm dying of thirst. Don't you think that I could go in and ask for a drink of water, even though Mrs. Hedberg is sick?"

"Yes, I suppose that would be all right," said Oscar. "The maid certainly can't refuse you that. Hurry up. I'll wait here."

Rasmus ran back. He climbed up the veranda steps and frightened the poor sparrows, who quickly scattered in all directions. He knocked on the outside door but didn't get any answer, so he went into the entrance hall. There were three doors. He picked the middle one and knocked again, but there was no answer. He hesitated for a moment, then opened the door and walked in.

An old lady was sitting in an easy chair and she stared at him as if he had been a ghost. The maid who had just chased them was standing there too, staring at him in a funny way.

Rasmus felt uncomfortable. "Could I please have a drink of water?" he asked shyly.

The old lady didn't take her eyes off him. She just sat there as if she were paralyzed, but then she seemed to make an effort and said, "Anna-Stina, give the boy some water."

Anna-Stina didn't seem particularly willing, but she disappeared into the kitchen and Rasmus was left alone with Mrs. Hedberg—the old lady couldn't be anyone else. He squirmed uncomfortably. Why did she keep on staring at him like that? She looked terrified. And why wasn't she in bed when she was sick?

"Are you very sick?" he said at last when he no longer could stand her staring.

"No, I'm not sick." It sounded as if she could hardly get the words out.

Wasn't she sick? Why had the maid lied and said that she was?

Anna-Stina came back with a mug of water, which she handed him sullenly. It was fresh, good water and he drank gratefully. While he was drinking his eyes looked around the room. This was a distinguished home, such as he had never seen before at close range. There were a beautiful red plush sofa, and easy chairs also covered in red plush, and a round table of fine, glossy wood, and a bureau with trimmings that looked like gold. The rug was a soft blend of colors and there was a fine, dark velvet drapery hanging over the door that led to the next room. Next to it was a beautiful stairway leading to the upper floor.

But there was something funny about that drapery. It *moved*, and it wasn't his imagination. Rasmus looked down at the floor. A shoe was sticking out under the edge of the drapery, a light tan shoe with an edge of black patent leather.

Funny habits they had in gentlefolks' houses! There definitely was a man behind that drapery. It was really no business of Rasmus'. Maybe they were playing a game of hide-and-seek in here. But what disturbed him was Mrs. Hedberg's eyes. He had never seen eyes so full of fear. She kept on staring toward the drapery as if something terrible were lurking behind it.

Maybe Anna-Stina felt sorry for Mrs. Hedberg, because now she made herself an errand to the door and on her way she straightened out the drapery so that it hid the shoe. Or maybe Anna-Stina didn't want Rasmus to know that a man was standing there?

Some of Mrs. Hedberg's fear came over him. He had the definite feeling that something unpleasant was happening. He was anxious to get away from this fine room with its drawn shades and staring, terrified eyes and unknown horrors behind the draperies. He wanted to get back out into the sunshine and to Oscar.

"Thank you for the water," he said and gave Anna-Stina back the mug as he walked toward the door.

"Do you have to go? Perhaps you could—"

This was Mrs. Hedberg's desperate voice behind him. Rasmus turned around and looked at her.

"What did you say?"

"Nothing. Perhaps you'd better go."

Rasmus left, puzzled and worried. Perhaps she meant that he could help her in some way?

He told Oscar everything and asked what he thought of it.

"Now don't you start telling me stories about bandits," said Oscar.

"Something was wrong in there. I'm sure of it."

They kept walking, but when they were out of sight of the villa Oscar stopped and scratched his head thoughtfully.

"We can't leave without at least trying to find out what sort of game they're playing. Come, we're going back!"

Quietly they slipped back through the gate. But instead of taking the garden path which led up to the villa, they crept behind the currant bushes so that they came to the back of the house.

There was no sign of life in any of the windows. But it gave them a creepy feeling to know that perhaps someone was standing inside peering out at them through the closed curtains.

"It's as quiet as a tomb around here," whispered Oscar.

"How are we going to find out what's happening behind those curtains? Can you tell me that?"

"We have to get inside, somehow."

"And how are we going to manage that?"

Rasmus was quiet for a while. "If we could somehow get in upstairs, that stairway would be a perfect place from which to see what is going on. We could lie flat on our stomachs up there and listen to what they were saying in the room with the drapery."

But Oscar shook his head. "It's dangerous business to trespass in other people's houses, especially for a tramp like me. Besides, I can't get in."

"But I can," Rasmus whispered eagerly. He pointed to an open window on the upper floor. It was probably in a closet, for it was so small and narrow that a big fellow like Oscar couldn't possibly squeeze through it. But Rasmus could manage. If Rasmus could be said to have a specialty, it was climbing trees, and a branch of one of the old maples stretched over the roof of the villa. With a trained eye he estimated the distance between the branch and the window. It wasn't more than three feet. He could manage that like nothing at all.

"You scare the life out of me," said Oscar. "It's dangerous. I can't let you do that."

"It's the only way," said Rasmus. "Help me to get up in the tree."

Rasmus was afraid of many things. He was afraid of being beaten, he was afraid of people, he had been afraid of the Hawk, he used to be afraid of getting involved in fights with some of the bigger boys at the orphanage, and that he would displease the teacher so that she would punish him. He was afraid to be alone in the dark—as a matter of fact he was afraid of being alone at all. But he had amazing physical courage. If it was a question of climbing or jumping or diving, it didn't make any difference how risky it looked—his skinny little frame had exaggerated confidence in its own ability and there wasn't a speck of fear in him. Therefore he refused to listen to Oscar's protests.

"Just help me into the maple," was his reply.

The lowest branches were too high for him to reach.

"You scare me to death," said Oscar. But he lifted Rasmus as if he had been a glove and heaved him up so that he was able to get hold of a branch. Rasmus grabbed it and pulled himself up. His arms, his legs, his fingers, and his toes were ready and eager for the job before him.

But Oscar was still afraid. He stood in the shadow of the maple and looked deeply worried as he saw his small friend disappearing through the little window.

7. Rasmus Investigates

Rasmus climbed into a clothes closet as big as a room. There was a stuffed parrot on a shelf and it would have been fun to examine it. But right now there was no time for parrots. He hesitated in front of the closed closet door. What would happen if he opened it? What was beyond it?

He opened the door a fraction of an inch. The slightest sound could give him away. It seemed like an eternity before he got the crack wide enough so that he could squeeze through it. Then he stood still and held his breath, listening, not daring to move. Only his eyes were quickly taking in the room he had come into.

This was another of those beautifully furnished rooms. There was a puffy sofa covered with chintz, an old grandfather clock ticking slowly and heavily, and a tall potted palm. And there were the stairs that led down to the ground floor.

From down below he heard a stifled cry. It was a terrifying sound which made his heart beat harder than ever. But he didn't have time to be afraid. He had to get over to the stairs to see what was happening.

As yet he couldn't see. He only kept hearing terrible

noises. Now someone was crying in a helpless way and some-one else was quickly walking across the floor. At times there was dead silence, and during those moments all he heard was the muted ticking of the clock which sounded more ominous than any of the other noises.

Gradually he inched himself closer to the staircase. First he tried every floor board to make sure it didn't squeak. When all was quiet downstairs he stood motionless, hardly daring to breathe, but cleverly made use of every noise from down below to cover the sound of his movements. Finally he had almost reached the steps. Then he noiselessly slid down to the floor and crawled the last bit on his stomach over to the railing. Now he was able to peek through the bars.

He had been right. It was a perfect place from which to watch. He couldn't see the whole room, but he could see Mrs. Hedberg. She was sitting there exactly as before and it was she who was crying. Anna-Stina was standing beside her, stroking her hand as if to calm her. And from the corner of the room that he couldn't see, a man came forward—no, there were two men, and they were masked! Both of them wore black masks and one of them was wearing those shoes that had been sticking out from under the drapery a while ago.

From the big clock behind him came a queer buzzing noise, and a wave of terror shot through Rasmus. Then he realized that it was only preparing to strike. The ten heavy "bongs" made Rasmus feel almost as if he were making the noise himself, and he prayed that those black-faced men

wouldn't come up the stairs and silence both him and the clock.

"No, no, not the bureau," Mrs. Hedberg was moaning.

No one answered her. The man at the bureau, the one with the shoes, began to pull out the drawers and scrabble through them.

Just then Rasmus felt something touching him. Someone was right behind him! He wanted to scream with terror; he wanted to die on the spot. But it was only a little black kitten, rubbing itself against his leg.

He adored kittens, but why did this little black rascal have to pick this of all times to come around purring like a machine? He tried to chase it away by giving it a gentle kick, but the kitten was stubborn. Here was someone to rub against and to purr to, and that's what it felt like doing right now. In one jump it was back at Rasmus again. This time it stroked itself against Rasmus' face, leaped around him, purred more happily than ever, and tucked its tail right into Rasmus' ear.

Rasmus was beside himself. To think that a cat couldn't understand that something terrible was happening under its own roof, but only purred and carried on, although its mistress was crying in anguish down there! He grabbed the kitten and gave it a rougher shove. The kitten landed on the floor a bit farther away and sat looking at Rasmus with wounded dignity. Then it turned around and walked off with its tail proudly in the air, making it quite clear that it wasn't going to take that sort of treatment from anyone.

Now Mrs. Hedberg's moans became louder. "No, no, not

the necklace," she begged. "Take everything else, but not the necklace. It's for my daughter."

The man at the bureau let the gold chain slide slowly between his fingers as if he hadn't heard Mrs. Hedberg. Then he put the necklace into his pocket and continued his search. The other man was standing at the door and Rasmus noticed that he had a gun in his hand which he pointed in the direction of Anna-Stina and Mrs. Hedberg.

It was awful! In anguish, Rasmus grabbed the bars of the railing. Then the most dreadful thing happened. A piece of the molding was loose. It could have been that way for a long time, even since before Rasmus was born. But during all these years it had stayed in place—until now. Until Rasmus happened to touch it at just the worst of all possible moments.

With a clatter it landed right behind the man at the bureau. He turned, drawing his pistol. "Who is up there?" he shouted with a voice like a whiplash.

Help, help, thought Rasmus in panic. Oscar, come and help me!

"There is no one up there," said Anna-Stina.

"Do pieces of wood rain down here all by themselves? You can't make me believe that." With his pistol cocked he cautiously started to climb the stairs.

Half out of his wits, Rasmus had slid backward, and when he heard the man coming up the steps he threw himself behind the sofa. Of all the games of hide-and-seek he had played in his life, this was the worst. The sofa was no good as a hiding place, but there was no time to look for anything

else. He could only lie still where he was and listen to the
steps coming nearer and nearer, and a more terrifying sound
he had never heard in all his life. For a moment there wasn't
a sound. The man was probably trying to decide from which
direction the attack would be coming, if an enemy was hiding up there.

The poor enemy wasn't prepared for any attack at all. He
was wishing himself far away, wishing that he had never
got himself into this, wishing that Oscar would come and
save him. But not even Oscar could save him now.

Those ominous steps came closer and closer. Now the
man was so close that Rasmus could see those ghastly
shoes with the black patent-leather edging. . . . Help!

Help did come from a very unexpected quarter!

The little black kitten had been playing with the filmy
curtains which were hanging at the window and swaying
so amusingly in the wind. He had been forbidden to hang
by his claws in the curtains, but it was fun and the kitten
was very happy. Then right beside him he saw a pair of boy's
feet with toes wiggling nervously back and forth. This was
even more fun than the curtains. With a joyous leap he
landed on his victim and sunk his sharp little claws into him.
He clawed and bit and made believe that the big toe was a
rat. Why didn't the boy think this was a wonderful game
too?

But he didn't. He took the poor little kitty in his hard fists
and threw it straight across the floor so that it landed right
in front of the feet of another person who didn't want to
play either. The person only said, "Darned cat," in a most

insulting way and disappeared down the stairs before the kitten even had a chance to sniff him over.

Rasmus lay motionless behind the sofa, his heart pounding. Of all the animals in the world, the cat was still the best, and of all cats this little black kitten was number one. It was the kitten that had saved him. The stupid man thought it was that "darned cat" who had knocked down the molding and that was oh, so lucky for Rasmus.

Rasmus didn't dare to leave his hiding place, but he strained his ears to hear what was going on downstairs. Mrs. Hedberg wasn't crying any longer. There wasn't a sound from her. Instead he heard Anna-Stina's frightened voice saying, "Merciful heaven! I think the old lady has fainted. I think she's sick. Hilding, what shall I do?"

"That's your business."

It was the one with the shoes who answered. Never before had Rasmus heard such a cold, cruel voice.

And Anna-Stina! Oscar was right. That maid *was* a shrew. She was a friend of the gangsters, there was no doubt about that.

"Hilding, I'm going to call the doctor," said Anna-Stina, and now she sounded really frightened.

"I advise you not to do that," said the cruel voice. "Besides, I've cut the telephone connection."

"Yes, but if Mrs. Hedberg is dying—" cried Anna-Stina.

"Shut up. You will get neither the doctor nor the sheriff before tonight, and don't you forget that!"

"But how am I going to explain—"

"Say that the old lady was so sick that you didn't dare leave her alone."

"I'm scared," said Anna-Stina. "I don't want any part of this."

You poor fool, thought Rasmus. This is a fine time to think of that. What wicked people there were in this world! Rasmus had a warm heart and he felt so terribly sorry for Mrs. Hedberg. Oh, if only he were big and strong! Then he would be able to take those gangsters by the scruff of the neck instead of having to lie here hiding like a coward.

They were in an awful hurry down there now. He heard the door close and then Anna-Stina's silly voice when she was left alone.

"Please, Mrs. Hedberg, wake up! Please."

Pale and trembling, Rasmus joined Oscar a few minutes later.

"At last!" said Oscar. "At last!"

Rasmus interrupted him. "Did you see them?" he whispered tensely.

Oscar shook his head. "I haven't seen a soul since you left. Golly, how I've been sweating!"

"You didn't see them," said Rasmus and his voice fell. Oscar should have been on the look-out and maybe he would have got a glimpse of the robbers unmasked.

"You should have been *watching*," said Rasmus. "What have you been doing all this time?"

"I've been sweating it out, I told you," said Oscar.

8. A Pair of Light Tan Shoes

"What are we going to do now?" Rasmus asked anxiously when he had told Oscar all that had happened.

Oscar kept shaking his head. He looked worried. " 'This week is certainly starting out well,' said the one who was about to be hanged on Monday! I don't know what we can do."

The world was certainly a terribly wicked place. They had retreated to a deserted pine hill right outside the village to hold a council of war. Rasmus was lying on his back in a sunny sand depression looking up at the little white puffs of cloud through the tops of the pine trees that were slowly swaying above him. He was distressed when he thought of poor Mrs. Hedberg. Perhaps at this moment she lay dying alone with her evil maid, the two masked men having disappeared with her necklace, no one knew where.

"We'll go to the sheriff," said Rasmus.

Oscar looked even more worried than before. "Then he'll surely put me in the jug. He'll think that I was involved in the Sandoe business as well as this with old Mrs. Hedberg."

"But if you tell him you're innocent?"

"Ah yes, if I tell him that I didn't do it, he'll let me go

free just like that, eh? You don't know what it's like to be
a vagabond. No, I don't dare go to the sheriff."

He scratched his neck thoughtfully. "But maybe we could
write to him. Can you write?"

"Pretty well, I think," said Rasmus.

"Then you write because I'm such a bad speller."

Oscar took a stubby pencil from his vest pocket and tore
a page from his notebook where he had written down the
words to his songs. The paper was badly crumpled—it
seemed as if the book had been lying out in the rain. But it
was still possible to write on it, and Rasmus wrote what
Oscar dictated:

Mrs. Hedberg in the green house has had something teribul
happen to her. The doctor has to go there and to the sheriff
too but please hurry asks a friend of widdos and orfans.
That awful maid is also mixed up in it.

Then they left their peaceful lair and started back to town.
Once again Rasmus crept behind the sheriff's privet hedge;
he threw the paper tied to a stone through the open window.
It made a thud on the floor and Rasmus ran back to Oscar,
who was waiting for him around the corner. Now they had
done what they could for Mrs. Hedberg and had to start
thinking of themselves.

"How long does it take before you starve to death?" Rasmus wanted to know. He felt as if he were well on the way.
It was already way past lunchtime and all he had had to
eat during this terrible morning was a sandwich and a piece
of butterscotch.

"Now we really have to make 'The Lion's Bride' work

for us if we're going to get anything to eat," said Oscar. "Not that I feel like singing now, but we just have to."

"The Lion's Bride" was wonderful when it came to earning money for food. For a few hours they went from house to house, playing and singing. Rasmus forgot the wickedness of the world and his own hunger in his delight with the pennies and five-cent pieces that rained over them.

People seemed to like Oscar's songs. They willingly parted with a few coins to hear about ladies being clawed to death by lions and abandoned by their faithless swains, and shot with guns so that they bathed in their own blood.

"Sad things do happen," sang Oscar, and the sadder the happenings, the more pleased was his audience, it seemed.

At the first sound from the accordion the maids abandoned the dishes in the kitchen and leaned out of the windows. They winked at Oscar and gladly gave him bits of money because the sun was shining and because they were going to meet their own faithful swains when evening came. Even the fine ladies looked out from their drawing-room windows, laughed and hummed the songs, and sent their children out with coins wrapped in paper. Rasmus collected the money, elated. What a wonderful profession, to be a wandering minstrel! "That's what I'm going to be when I grow up," he said to Oscar later.

"Is that so? Do you like to sing that much?"

"No, but I like money that much," said Rasmus truthfully. At the orphanage no one had ever had any money.

"But you shouldn't be picking up five-cent pieces all your life. There are other professions where you can make more money."

Rasmus tucked the last harvest of coins into Oscar's pocket. "But you see, I think I like five-cent pieces best of all." But a sad expression came over his face. He didn't want to think about what he would do when he grew up because then he would have to think about what would become of him in the meantime. What would happen to him when he no longer could be on the road with Oscar? Suppose no one in the world wanted to give him a home?

He decided to put it out of his mind and take each day as it came and be happy about the nice things that were happening at this very moment.

"If you like money so much, you should have some," said Oscar, and he pressed two coins into Rasmus' hand.

Rasmus flushed with delight. He took Oscar by the hand and bowed as he had been taught to do when he was given something. He couldn't say a word for a long time, but finally he awkwardly pulled Oscar's sleeve and said, "You are the best tramp in the world, Oscar." Never before in his life had he been given anything, so a gift was a sort of miracle to him which proved that someone cared. The coins meant that Oscar liked him and he walked along happily, fingering them. They made him feel so rich in many ways.

"Oh, I'm the way most tramps are," Oscar said. "Nice sometimes and mean sometimes. Come, let's go to Hultman's and buy some eats!"

The thought of food made Rasmus weak and his knees almost gave way when he went into Hultman's Delicatessen. There was a heavenly smell of things to eat. Red and brown sausages were piled high on the counter. A beautiful headcheese and a hickory-smoked ham were competing for attention with liverwurst and all kinds of cheeses. A special shelf was filled with all kinds of candy. This splendid empire was ruled over by a friendly grocer who came hurrying out as soon as he heard the tinkling of the bell, eager to serve them. He had small, fat hands with black-rimmed nails, but oh, how deftly he sliced the marvelous ham and the luscious pink sausage, and how quickly he got together the bread and butter and cheese and tobacco for Oscar while keeping up a friendly stream of conversation the whole time!

"Summer really seems to be here at last," he said as he handed Oscar the tobacco. Then he turned to Rasmus and said something still nicer. "How would you like to have a piece of chocolate?" Without further ado he took a chocolate bar from the shelf—one of the smallest, but still! It was wrapped in red foil and it glittered like a precious stone between his fat little fingers. "Here you are," he said.

Rasmus shook hands with him and bowed again and Oscar said, "Now let's see if we have enough for a couple of root beers, then I think that will be all."

It was already past three o'clock and they decided to retrace their steps to the pine hill and eat their lunch in peace and quiet.

The news about the hold-up probably hadn't got around yet. The little village seemed peaceful and the streets were still in the afternoon sun when Oscar and Rasmus came walking along Brook Street.

"Just wait until people get wind of what's happened. Then you'll see this place come to life," said Oscar. "But that fathead of a sheriff probably hasn't found the letter yet.

It isn't enough to throw rocks at him. He probably needs a bomb right on his noodle to wake him up."

The village inn was situated down at the river in the midst of a lovely little garden. At this time of day people were sitting around the small white garden tables having their afternoon tea and coffee.

"I know you're hungry, Rasmus," Oscar said, "but here we have to play even if we pass out while we're at it. We couldn't possibly miss out on so much cash."

He got out the accordion and they took their places at a respectful distance from the guests. These were mostly ladies, rich and beautiful, with big hats and lace collars, and Rasmus just couldn't stop looking at them as they sat there eating cinnamon buns and Danish pastry. He would have liked someone exactly like that for a mother—if he could find someone who really wanted him.

He already knew that wouldn't be so easy. They looked expectantly at him, but only because they wanted to hear him sing—him and Oscar, but mostly Oscar. There probably wasn't a single one among them who was thinking she would like to have him for her own.

Rasmus sighed. But now Oscar had started to play and Rasmus had to help with the singing.

> "Have you heard the terrible news?
> If not, we'll tell it to you:
> The king of North America
> Has been shot, shot right in two."

Rasmus found it easy to learn both words and tunes, and after his few hours of wandering around, singing at the houses, he knew all Oscar's blood-curdling songs. "Diddle diddle do dum dum," he sang as an accompaniment to Oscar while his eyes wandered among the ladies to decide which he would pick for a mother if he had the choice. At a table right next to him sat a chubby lady who was probably the owner of this inn, because now and then she would call out something to the waitresses. But mostly she talked with the two gentlemen at her table. She put her head to one side and seemed so anxious to please them and kept laughing the whole time for no reason at all. She said, "Please Mr. Lif, do have another cookie," and "May I serve you some more coffee, Mr. Liander?" It sounded as if there were nothing in the world she would rather do.

The gentlemen, Mr. Lif and Mr. Liander, were very well dressed. They wore white straw hats and had neat little mustaches, both of them, and one of them even wore a flower in his buttonhole.

"Diddle diddle do dum dum," sang Rasmus, his soprano blending effectively with Oscar's deep bass.

. . . and they wore striped summer suits with narrow trousers and one of them had shoes which—which—shoes which—

"That the king of North America—"

Rasmus stopped dead in the middle of the song. Mr. Lif had light tan shoes on, *shoes edged with patent leather!*

All the anguish of the morning came back over him. He remembered Mrs. Hedberg's moans and the terrible steps approaching when he was lying behind the sofa. It was exactly that kind of shoes that had come so menacingly close to him. No wonder he couldn't sing when he saw shoes like that again!

Even Oscar's black look, asking what on earth had got into him, didn't spur him on. He just stood there stupidly, unable to move. Lif might be a completely innocent person who just happened to have the same kind of terrible gangster shoes, but nevertheless Rasmus was unable to sing any more. He got gooseflesh when he saw those shoes. He wasn't even hungry any more.

"Listen, Hilding, tomorrow we'll have to start our fishing a little earlier," said the other gentleman at the table.

Hilding! Mr. Lif's name was Hilding! His name was the same as the robber and he had shoes like the robber!

"Yes, we should make good use of the days we have left," said Mr. Lif.

He had a voice just like the robber's, too!

"But you'll stay to the end of the week in any case?" said the chubby lady anxiously.

"Yes, we plan to. We feel so at home here."

But Rasmus didn't feel at home at all. He felt as if he were going to pass out at any moment. As soon as Oscar had finished singing about the king of North America, Rasmus frantically tugged at his sleeve to get him away from there.

"And what are we going to do now?" said Rasmus. They were back in their sand hole again. The world was still wicked and Rasmus had been sick behind a tree. Food didn't want to stay in his stomach when there was so much to worry about.

Oscar sucked on his pipe for a long time, deep in thought.

"Well, I guess the only thing left for me to do is to go to the sheriff and tell him I *think* those two fancy gentlemen at the inn robbed Mrs. Hedberg. But how to get the sheriff to *believe* it, that's another problem."

He knocked the ashes from his pipe and put his rucksack on. "My legs are sort of unwilling to head for the sheriff's office. But come on, let's go."

"May heaven help us!" said Rasmus. "That is what Aunt Olga used to say when there was an inspection at Vaesterhaga, and the sheriff is probably much worse than inspection."

"But it's going to be a long time before I come back to these parts again," said Oscar. "Such a black den of iniquity. It's better to stick to the real country where there are no robbers!"

The little village which Oscar with some exaggeration called a den of iniquity had undergone a marked change in their absence. People were now standing in small groups on the street corners and you could see from a distance that they were talking about something special. It wasn't hard to figure out what it was.

"I'd give a lot to know what they're saying, before I go to the sheriff," mumbled Oscar. He handed Rasmus a few pennies. "Run over and get some candy, and keep both your ears open."

"I'll find out what's going on," said Rasmus. He ran up the street until he found a grocery store. He could see through the glass pane in the door that there were quite a few people inside. That was just fine. He would have to wait a while before his turn came and in the meantime he would keep his ears open. Then he would buy candy! Filled with expectation he opened the door.

A few minutes later he came running back to Oscar in wild panic, white as a sheet. "Oscar, we've got to get out of here fast!"

"What's the matter? Where's the fire?"

Rasmus grabbed Oscar's hand and started pulling him. "Oscar, Anna-Stina has told the sheriff that you were the one who attacked them!"

Oscar opened his eyes wide and his face flushed with indignation. "Me! But she doesn't even know me! She doesn't even know my name!"

"She said that a tramp came around playing the accordion and had a boy with him. When he finished he came in the house and threatened her and Mrs. Hedberg with a pistol and took Mrs. Hedberg's emerald necklace."

"That woman is a shrew, and if I had her here I would shove those lies back down her cursed throat. But old Mrs. Hedberg? What does she say?"

"They think she's going to die. She can't say anything because she is lying as if she were dead. Her heart is hardly beating at all. The doctor has been there!"

The veins at Oscar's temples started to swell. He was red with rage and he banged his forehead with his fist. "Well that's just great! Then that girl can get away with all her lies and the sheriff will believe every word."

Rasmus kept pulling at his sleeve. "Oscar, please come. We have to get out of here!"

"That's what you think!" said Oscar furiously. "I'm

going to put that girl up against the wall in the sheriff's office and then she can say I did it if she dares!"

The tears welled up in Rasmus' eyes and he sobbed, "Oscar, the sheriff will arrest you. You said yourself that he has no use for tramps. And if he throws you in jail—" He stopped. He didn't dare think of what would happen if Oscar landed in jail.

Apparently Oscar didn't dare to think about it either. All anger suddenly left him and he stood there, utterly dejected, his arms dangling, looking sad and worried.

"Yes, you're right. If I go to the sheriff, I'm done for." He grabbed Rasmus by the arm. "Quick, we'll get out of here before it's too late," he said, pulling the boy with him into the street. "That is, if it isn't already too late," he mumbled.

To get away from this place where every person was on the look-out for the tramp with the accordion would perhaps not be so easy. But luck was with them. They managed to slip away through deserted back streets and get outside the town limits to the peaceful open road.

"We're running like a pair of murderers," said Oscar, and he gritted his teeth.

Rasmus slowed down. He was so out of breath that he could hardly get the words out. "And you're innocent, Oscar!"

"As innocent as a bride."

"So am I," said Rasmus.

"So you are," said Oscar. He turned around and looked bitterly at the little town with its roofs rising above the summer greenery. "Den of iniquity," he said. It was good to be on the road again.

Rasmus felt the same way. On the road there were no thieves and bandits. Everything was peaceful. Wildflowers grew in profusion along the ditches and the sweet scent of clover rose from the fields. The sun had gone down and the silence was heavy as it often is before a storm. Gray, billowy clouds sailed across the sky like ships at sea. Lonely and empty the road stretched out before them as far as the eyes could see, and at the horizon, where earth and sky met, it seemed to continue on straight into heaven.

"Where are we going now?" Rasmus asked.

"To a place where we can hide," said Oscar, "the like of which you've probably never seen."

9. The Hiding Place

They came to a tiny deserted village by the sea. There were five little gray houses nestled in the spaces between the rocks, which were also gray. Here even the sea had turned gray as the summer day faded, and clouds, leaden and heavy with rain, hung over this village where no one lived. This was a good hiding place. Here was only abandonment and silence and the grayest desolation.

"Oscar, where are the people who used to live in the houses?" Rasmus asked.

Oscar was sitting on a rock. He had taken off his shoes and socks and with a look of relief on his face was spreading his toes out in the coolness of the evening.

"They emigrated to America, the whole bunch of them."

"Why didn't they want to live here any longer?"

"Their life was probably too poor and miserable and gray in these houses—not enough fish in the sea, and those little patches of land probably couldn't produce enough to live on."

Rasmus nodded. That was something he understood. He knew full well how terrible it was to be poor. "But they certainly had good swimming here," he said as he looked down

into the transparent water whirling around the rocks. "They probably wouldn't find anything like that where they were going."

"Oh, I suppose they could swim in the clearest lake in Minnesota if they wanted to," said Oscar.

Rasmus smiled. "The clearest lake in Minnesota"—that sounded so picturesque. He would like to see it sometime as well as all the other lakes and mountains and rivers in the world. He tried to imagine those people walking around over there looking for the clearest lake in Minnesota. Perhaps they were thinking of the cliffs at home and wondering if anyone was living in their little gray houses by the sea.

"I'm going to take a look," he said and ran over to the nearest cottage. He wanted to see if there were any remains of the Minnesota travelers in there.

Through a broken window he was able to peek into a miserable little cottage with ceiling beams blackened by smoke and a sooty open fireplace. It must have been ages since anyone had made a fire and cooked over it. Rasmus felt sorry for houses where no one lived. They seemed so lonesome—as if they were longing for people to come and make themselves at home, build a fire in the fireplace, put on the coffeepot, and make breakfast for their children.

He brushed away a few glass splinters from the window-sill and climbed in. There were dead leaves and other rubbish lying around and the floor creaked under his bare feet. He went to the fireplace and peeked up under the hood. When had the last fire been made here? Oh well, he would never know. But once this cottage had been a real home. How wonderful if it would be again and he could climb in and live in it! But if it were a real home with people in it he would of course only be allowed to stand at the kitchen door as tramps usually do. They would have their own children and wouldn't need a boy from an orphanage. But it was nice to pretend just the same.

He ran to the window. "Oscar, this is where we're going to stay," he shouted.

"Yes, at least for the night," Oscar called back from the cliff. "For a while I want to keep out of sight, and besides, I'm sore at everybody."

Rasmus was having a good time in the Minnesota emigrant's empty house. He ran up and down the stairs and in and out of the porch and kitchen and the tiny rooms. He was wondering which house to chose and finally decided on the one that was in the most sheltered position and the least ravaged by wind and water.

It had a narrow little kitchen and a tiny room just like the other houses, and it also had a steep, rickety stairway leading up to a miserable attic and attic room. But it was a house and they could make believe that it was a real home. He could almost imagine that Oscar was his father, and if he really gave free rein to his imagination he could imagine that Oscar was a rich grocer and not a tramp at all. Unfortunately there was no grocer's wife, but he could pretend that she had gone on a trip, perhaps to Minnesota, and would soon come back home carrying a lace parasol and wearing a blue hat with feathers. She would be very pretty and she would bring him and Oscar fine presents. Then the three of them would live in the house and be rich, very rich.

But a home has to have furniture—tables and sofas and rugs and curtains, like Mrs. Hedberg's. Rasmus wished for furniture so intensely that it seemed as if it would rise from the floor. But to imagine mahogany tables and sofas upholstered in gay prints in this bare room was a superhuman feat even for Rasmus. Then he remembered having seen a dump at the roadside a bit farther down, and ran over there. People throw so much stuff on a dump. Maybe there was something he could use for furniture.

He came back with an empty sugar crate, a couple of margarine boxes, and a whole lot of other things he had picked up. The sugar crate would make a fine table after he had washed it off in the sea. But first the cottage had to be swept.

He broke off a branch from a tree and with that he cleared out as much as he could of the trash. Then he brought his table in. On it he put an empty bottle which made a fine vase for the almond blossoms he had picked. The margarine boxes had turned into chairs. Rugs and curtains he just had to imagine.

Oscar had gone off into the woods to find spruce branches for them to sleep on, and when he came back Rasmus called out to him, "Over here with the bedding!"

Oscar didn't have much imagination, but he still realized that he was coming into a very well-furnished room. He stood in the doorway, his arms filled with fragrant spruce boughs, and wiped his feet. "I'd better clean off my hoofs before I come in," he said. "Just tell me where you want me to put the swansdown bolsters."

"Put them over there," said Rasmus, pointing to a corner of the room.

Oscar obediently spread out the spruce branches to form a bed. Rasmus was very pleased with the effect. The green brightened up the room considerably. They could use it as both a rug and a bed, and it made the whole room cosy.

"It's lucky you got everything in order," said Oscar, "because it's going to pour any minute."

Almost before the words were out of his mouth the rain came down in torrents, splashing against the broken windowpanes and pounding on the roof. The room had quite suddenly become dark, but Rasmus felt at home. The rain made it still cosier.

"Should we perhaps have something to eat?" said Rasmus hesitatingly. They had eaten something in a hurry at the roadside, but not enough. Besides, they had to make use of their table. Oscar still had most of the supplies they had bought at Hultman's and he laid out the bread and butter and cheese and ham and salami on the sugar crate. Each of them sat down on a margarine box, eating contentedly and listening to the rain. Rasmus was thinking, Never will I forget this—the wonderful time we had when we were eating and it was pouring outside.

He couldn't tell Oscar that he was pretending that they had a real home and that Oscar was a prosperous grocer with a wife in a blue hat with feathers who was away on a trip. But he looked longingly at his companion over a salami sandwich and said, "Suppose you were my father and we lived together in a house!"

"Yes, wouldn't that be just dandy—a tramp for a father."

Rasmus was quiet for a few minutes. It was true that he wanted his parents to be rich and attractive. A tramp wasn't exactly what he had in mind. Oh, if Oscar had only been a wealthy, handsome grocer!

The rain stopped as suddenly as it had started. The two vagabonds had finished their supper and now made themselves comfortable on their spruce branches in the corner. Oscar took the piece of blanket which he used to wrap around the accordion and put it over Rasmus.

My father, thought Rasmus, is wrapping a red satin comforter around me because my mother is in Minnesota and can't be with me. She is bathing in the clearest lake and is writing letters home saying, "I'll be coming home soon and I'll have a lot of fine presents with me. Tuck Rasmus in well at night in the red satin comforter. I'll be home soon."

It was getting darker outside. The wind, which had been holding its breath during the rain, now came from the sea in gusts. A storm was coming up. The waves splashed against the rocks more violently and the wind was tugging at the slender birches outside.

Many strange sounds were beginning to come to life in the cottage. From the broken windows came peeping, whining noises. Somewhere a door banged without stopping until finally Oscar got annoyed. "Will that darned door ever stop banging? A body who is sleeping here won't have any trouble staying awake."

Rasmus didn't like all the creaking and squeaking. He was afraid. With wide-open eyes he lay in his corner, staring out into the darkness like a frightened animal.

"Maybe there are ghosts here," he whispered. "If the ghosts come and get us—"

But Oscar wasn't afraid. "If you see any ghosts, just tell them they can go and jump in the sea. Otherwise God's best friend will come and make ghost hash of them."

But Rasmus wasn't reassured. "Aunt Olga in the kitchen once saw a dog who had no head and sparks of fire came from his throat."

Oscar yawned. "Aunt Olga in the kitchen had no head either, it seems. There are no such things as ghosts."

"There certainly are," said Rasmus. "Do you know what Big Peter says? He says that if you run around the church twelve times at midnight they will come and take you."

"I think they would be right to take you. Why on earth should you be running around the church in the middle of the night? Anyone would have to be pretty weak in the head to do that and then he would have only himself to blame."

Oscar didn't want to talk about ghosts any more. He wanted to sleep. Rasmus was sleepy too, although he had had a nap in the sand hole, but all that sighing and squeaking kept him awake. Oscar was already snoring, but Rasmus lay there tense and listening.

Then he heard voices! Yes, it was definitely voices he heard! Old gray houses may sigh and creak in the night wind, but real voices could only mean ghosts. With a pitiful cry he threw himself on Oscar. "Oscar, now the ghosts are coming. I hear them talking."

Oscar sat up among the spruce branches, wide awake. "Talking? Who is talking?" He was on the alert, listening intently. Yes, Rasmus was right. Someone was talking close by.

"Dear me, that means the sheriff again," Oscar groaned. He crept up to the window on his knees and peered out into the darkness. Rasmus was behind him, frightened out of his wits and biting his nails in desperation.

"I'm for taking the dough and beating it," a voice was saying. A man was standing right outside the window, and it didn't sound like the sheriff.

"You'd better let me handle this," another voice said, and that voice Rasmus recognized. He would know Hilding Lif's voice among a thousand others. Rasmus held on to Oscar's arm. Lif and Liander were even worse than ghosts and sheriffs.

Now they were coming in. Help! They were in the kitchen and Rasmus heard the floor creaking under their steps. What were they doing here in the middle of the night and was there no place in the world where he and Oscar could get away from robbers?

The door between the kitchen and Rasmus' finely furnished room wasn't closed. There was a broad crack through which they could hear every word that was said in the kitchen.

"I think it's dangerous to wait any longer," said the voice which belonged to Liander. "I want to get out of here."

"No, no," said Lif. "We mustn't get jittery and spoil everything. It wouldn't be a good idea to skip out just when the old lady has lost her necklace. We'll stay the rest of the week at the inn. That will look good. Our conscience is clear, you see? We've never been to Sandoe. Otherwise we wouldn't be staying at the inn a few miles from there for almost two weeks. You see the point?"

"Yes I see it, all right," said Liander, "because you've said it at least fourteen times before. But I would like to take the dough and get out because I think we'll be sitting here with our good conscience until we're caught but good."

"It's going to be the way I said," said Lif. "We'll grab the dough on Saturday morning and then calmly take the two-o'clock train and no one will get any funny ideas about the necklace or anything."

It sounded as if the men were taking up some loose boards in the kitchen, and then they heard Lif saying, in a voice that purred, "It does my soul good to see so much dough." There was silence for a while, and then he continued: "My guess is that the necklace is also worth five or six thousand."

"I'd like to be rid of it," said Liander. "Sandoe worked out okay, but the business with Anna-Stina was no good. It's all right with me if you pick up with one of your discarded girl friends, but to do *business* with women—that's signing your own death warrant."

"Are you scared?" said Lif with a sneer.

"I'm not scared. It's just that I don't like this one bit. Suppose the old lady revives?"

"She won't. She has lived long enough as it is."

" '*If* she revives,' I said. Suppose she comes to and tells what happened and the sheriff gives Anna-Stina the third degree about that tramp. That stupid Anna-Stina, she should never have blamed it on the tramp, because if the sheriff finds out she has lied there, it won't take more than five minutes before he gets the truth out of her. Then it will only take five minutes more and we'll be stuck for Sandoe too."

"Take it easy," said Lif. "You've been nagging about that all day and I'm sick and tired of it. Anna-Stina isn't that dumb, and besides the old lady won't be talking any more."

Liander growled.

"And we sure have a good hiding place for the dough," Lif continued. "This is much better than digging the stuff down in the woods. It's easy to find, and in a place people would never think of looking."

"If you just don't find your way here by yourself before Saturday," said Liander sourly.

Lif flared up. "Don't you trust me?"

Liander laughed a dry, harsh laugh. " 'Don't you trust

me?' said the fox as he bit the head off the hen. Yes, I trust
you about the way you trust me."

Rasmus dug his nails into Oscar's arm. This was almost
more than he could take. It was ghastly to think that there
were people who wanted to do away with others and unbearable to have those horrible characters so close, only a
few feet away from them. He wished himself as far away
as possible. Still, the adventurous part of him wanted to stay
behind and see what would happen next. He heard them
banging around with the boards again. Now they were probably hiding the money. But just wait until they had left!

"Let's go," said Liander.

"Okay," said Lif.

Rasmus was already heaving a deep sigh of relief but then
Lif said something that made his blood run cold.

"I'm going to take a look around and see if I can find the
pipe I forgot here the last time. I think I put it on the windowsill in there."

"In there" could only mean the room where Oscar and
Rasmus were sitting huddled close together in their corner.
Rasmus pressed himself still closer to Oscar, so terrified
that his head was swimming. He felt the muscles in Oscar's
arms become tense and knew he was getting ready to fight.
But the gangsters had guns. This was really the end for
them!

There was the sound of quick footsteps. The door was
opened and the light from a flashlight fell across the floor.
In the middle of the room was Rasmus' fine furniture, but
the light quickly swept over the sugar crate. The gangster

didn't seem to think there was anything peculiar about it's being there. He wasn't at all surprised, but probably would be when he caught sight of Oscar and Rasmus. They pressed themselves still closer into their corner and waited. Oscar's muscles became still tenser. But then . . .

"Here's the pipe," said Liander's voice from the kitchen. "It's right here on the windowsill."

Lif turned around and went back. The threatening beam of light faded and he left the room without noticing the two in the corner. This was a pure miracle, because not even the darkest corner was really dark. But two tramps probably aren't noticed by someone looking for a pipe.

"That one sure was wearing blinders," said Rasmus when the gangsters had disappeared into the windy night and he dared to talk again.

"Come on," said Oscar, picking up his flashlight. "Now we'll take a look at that good hiding place which is so easy to find. This is going to be very interesting!"

They went into the kitchen and Rasmus was wild with excitement. In his imagination he saw a huge pit filled with gold and silver coins.

Oscar's flashlight traveled over the floor boards. He examined each one and tried with his foot to see if it was secure.

"This is it!" Eagerly he loosened a board next to the stove; he loosened another one and pointed his flashlight into the hole. A square piece of the earth underneath had been dug out and in its place was a big package well wrapped in oil cloth. Oscar opened it.

"Ah!" was all Rasmus could say. Piles of bills of large

denominations were stacked in neat rows—the whole pay-roll from the Sandoe factory! There were no gold and silver coins but Rasmus could tell by Oscar's almost frightened expression that this was money too.

"I didn't think there was so much of this stuff in the whole world," said Oscar. There were also a necklace and a gold chain with a pendant set with huge green stones. It was the most beautiful thing Rasmus had ever seen in his life, but of course he hadn't seen many beautiful things. A great wave of relief and pleasure came over him. "Now Mrs. Hedberg will get her necklace back. If she is still alive. . . ."

Oscar let the gold chain glide between his fingers. "I hope I'll have a chance to sing 'Every Forest Has Its Spring' for her once more," he said.

Rasmus was elated. "Tomorrow we'll go to the sheriff with the money and to Mrs. Hedberg with the necklace."

"No we don't. We have to be clever about this."

"But what else can we do?" said Rasmus.

"I'm not going to stick my nose into that beehive again. With lying maids and all the commotion and 'What did you do on Thursday, Oscar'—no sir! What we'll do is hide the stuff in a different place and write a new note to the sheriff saying, 'Please pick up the money before it's too late.' Then you and I will hit the road again and let the sheriff take care of the rest. That's what he's paid for. I haven't signed on as a sort of sheriff's assistant."

Oscar began to fill his rucksack with the stacks of bills. "If the sheriff catches me walking around with a whole bank on my back, I'll probably get life." He took the necklace and playfully put it around Rasmus' neck. "You're going

to be real fancy for once in your life. Now you look like
King Solomon himself in all his glory, except a bit more
freckled."

In the light of the flashlight King Solomon stood there,
all skinny arms and legs with emeralds around his neck.
"And straight hair," added Rasmus sadly. He tugged at the
necklace. He didn't want to have it on. But there was no
time to take it off. Because there they were again—the
voices!

10. The Chase

"Quick," whispered Oscar. "Let's get out of here fast." They ran toward the porch. But it was too late. Now the voices were close, right outside the door. There was no escape that way.

"The attic!" Oscar pushed Rasmus ahead of him up the narrow, steep stairs where Rasmus had been skipping up and down so gaily before. Now he stumbled and felt sick, and terrified of the two who were just now opening the outer door and coming into the dark house.

Oscar and Rasmus stopped dead in the stairway. They didn't dare move and hardly dared breathe, afraid that even a breath might give them away. Rasmus stared in panic at the two nightmarish black shadows down there. Oh, how he detested them!

"No, you're right. There were no boxes here the last time." That was Lif's voice. Now he was opening the door to the kitchen.

"And still you don't have the wits to speak up when you see a whole box factory," said Liander accusingly. "The boxes didn't get there by themselves. That much I should think you could figure out."

"I didn't think of it until afterward," said Lif. "You know how it is sometimes—you see something but you don't see it. And then, in a while—bang, it just dawns on you. Where on earth did those boxes come from?"

"See and don't see! We can't afford such talk in our business. But now we're getting the dough out of here!"

Ha! That's what you think, said Rasmus gleefully to himself. Despite his fear, he felt triumphant. But it was all wiped out the next moment with the cry of rage from the kitchen and the furious roar from Lif.

"After them, fast. They can't be far away."

They went tearing out like bloodhounds in search of the unknown enemy who had taken their loot, intending to demolish him when they laid their hands on him. But suddenly Lif stopped. "Wait. First we have to see if they're still in the house. There's no one down here. Maybe up in the attic."

He dashed up the stairs—right into Oscar's fist. With a moan he fell backward into Liander's arms. Rasmus moaned too as he stood behind Oscar's broad back, because he saw Liander pull out his terrible gun and heard him say in a voice shaking with rage, "If you move, I'll shoot."

Now Lif had got to his feet again. The beam of his flashlight caught the two on the stairs and he gasped when he saw King Solomon in all his glory. "The kid is wearing the necklace!" The robbers stared as if they hardly believed their eyes.

"Run, Rasmus!" shouted Oscar. He stood there, broad and tremendous, blocking the narrow stairs. "Run!" he shouted in a thundering voice.

Rasmus ran. Like a rat being chased he ran the rest of the way up the stairs and across the miserable attic room, where the wind was shaking the empty window frames so they rattled. Outside the window was the roof of the kitchen. He heaved himself over the window ledge. Climbing on roofs was something he was good at, and jumping too. It was a leap of about a dozen feet to the ground but he could have jumped from a church steeple if it had been necessary. He landed on his knees and felt pain, but he didn't have time to stop. He was a terrified rat, pursued by the cat. He already heard Lif coming around the corner to block him and he ran as if his life were at stake—in fact, he knew that it was.

Oh you Minnesota travelers, if you only knew what is happening in your gray house by the sea tonight! A terrified boy with emeralds around his neck is running between the houses with a robber hot on his trail. There is no one to help him. The gray houses are quiet and deserted. The windows are dead and silent. No friendly door is opened in the windy night. No kind voice calls through an open window, "Come in here. We'll hide you."

He is completely on his own, this barefoot boy in the striped orphanage shirt and patched homespun pants, with an emerald necklace around his neck, running, seeking protection behind the nearest house. This one once belonged to Peter Anderson, but the boy, so frantically running here many years after Peter Anderson's departure, doesn't know that. He stands still for a second, his heart pounding violently, trying to figure out in what direction to run. He doesn't have a second to lose because his pursuer is coming around the corner. The pursuer's hair is standing straight

up in the wind, and he is no longer a fine gentleman in a straw hat, but a desperate gangster who has to get hold of the boy, no matter what.

Rasmus runs in wild panic. He is fast, but his pursuer has longer legs and can run still faster. The pursuer is gaining on him. When Rasmus glances around he can see those long legs moving with terrifying speed and the hair standing straight up in the wind.

Next to Peter Anderson's house is Carl Nelson's, surrounded by a cluster of sheds. Rasmus stops behind Carl Nelson's old carpenter shed. He stands motionless, waiting for his enemy to pounce on him. Here he comes! But he races by. He doesn't notice the boy pressing himself close to the wall. Rasmus has a few seconds to catch his breath.

But the cat discovers the rat again. Lif sees his prey on the way back to Peter Anderson's house and goes after him. Rasmus runs, panting. He has a good head start, but in a contest with Lif he can't possibly win. He has to find a hiding place, quickly. Peter Anderson's house? He runs in there, but what sort of hiding place can he find in a completely empty house?

There is a woodbin. Many generations of children have played hide-and-seek here. They have crept into the woodbin and pulled the lid down over themselves. But no one has ever been in there in such a panic, waiting for a pair of cruel hands to come and pull him out from his hiding place. Now the trap has snapped shut on the rat. If Lif finds him here, he is done for.

Here he comes! Rasmus hears his steps in the kitchen, terribly close. Any minute he will lift the lid. But most likely Lif has never played hide-and-seek and doesn't know anything about woodbins, because he dashes into the room and up the stairs to the attic. He knows the boy must be somewhere in this house.

But Rasmus is already out of the woodbin and outside the house again. He hopes that he has fooled Lif this time. He prays frantically that he will not be discovered.

No such luck. Through the attic window Lif sees the

barefoot lad running across the yard, his legs moving like drumsticks. With two leaps down the stairs the gangster is after him, relentless as fate.

The chase continues along the old village street. In former times peaceful oxcarts trundled along here on their way to the barn with Peter Anderson's wheat and Carl Nelson's hay, and on summer nights the children rolled their hoops along. Never before has anyone had to run for his life on this street. Rasmus runs down toward the sea with Lif in hot pursuit. What is the boy going to do, jump in? Lif increases his speed. There has to be an end to this right now!

A dilapidated boat landing juts right out into the sea, and at the end of it is a half-collapsed boathouse. Rasmus runs out on the landing. It sways under him. It sways still more when Lif comes. But the gangster smiles triumphantly. The youngster is as good as caught. Running out on the landing was the most stupid thing he could have done. There is no way back. Now he's finished if he doesn't want to jump in and drown himself.

At the boathouse the landing makes a right angle. Rasmus keeps on running along the rickety planks. His shirt has come out of his pants during the chase and a blue-striped shirttail is the last thing Lif sees before Rasmus disappears behind the boathouse.

The landing creaks ominously as Lif comes running. Now, finally, that tough youngster will get what he deserves. Lif dashes after him around the corner of the boathouse. Suddenly the pounding footsteps are no longer heard. Instead there is a big splash. Mr. Lif doesn't even have time to shout before the salt waves wash over him. He tries, but only a little "blup" comes out.

For a second Rasmus is almost triumphant. Digging up potatoes wasn't the only thing he had learned at Vaesterhaga. He also learned to trip up an enemy.

Coughing and spitting, Lif comes to the surface in a blind rage. He scrambles up on the landing and Rasmus, panic-stricken, realizes that he will never get away this time. But he is going to do his utmost. He is going to run until he collapses. But that won't be long now, because his heart is pounding as if it would burst.

The chase goes back along the landing, along the village street, across Carl Nelson's front yard and into Peter Anderson's. It's just like being pursued in a nightmare. Now he's in the lead, but his enemy is gaining on him, relentless, sopping wet, ruthless. Rasmus will never make it.

Peter Anderson's potato cellar! Rasmus has been down there before when he was playing at house hunting and was making believe that he had fifty sacks of potatoes to make potato fritters with.

Completely at the end of his strength, he slips into the darkness of the cellar, hoping against hope that Lif isn't close enough to see him and won't think of looking here. It's a feeble little hope that quickly vanishes.

He hears someone grab hold of the door handle, and here comes Lif, wet and raging at the urchin who dares to put him through all this. Blindly he plunges into the cellar.

But at Vaesterhaga Rasmus has also learned another trick. Many a time he would hide inside a door and, when the

pursuer dashed in, quickly jump out behind him. This is
exactly what Rasmus does now. Lif hurtles past, and, quick
as a flash, Rasmus dodges out, bangs the cellar door, and
turns the rusty key. Not until he hears Lif's terrible roars
on the other side of the door does he realize what he has
done. He has locked his enemy in Peter Anderson's old potato cellar!

His legs are shaking. He is dead tired. He longs for Oscar.
But perhaps Oscar is dead. . . .

As fast as he can he runs back to "his" house. He ap-
proaches very cautiously. He doesn't know where Oscar is
or where Liander is. It is already dawn. Soon the sun will
rise over the Minnesota travelers' old village.

Rasmus throws himself down on his stomach in the grass
and inches himself over to the kitchen window. Slowly he
gets up on his knees and peers through the windowless
frame.

Liander was standing with his back against the window,
very close. Oscar was near the stove with his hands up.
Liander was holding his gun and had Oscar's rucksack at
his feet.

"Shoot," said Oscar. "One hobo more or less in the world
doesn't make any difference."

"You can just bet my fingers are itching to pull the trig-
ger," Liander said. "But I don't want to disappoint the
sheriff. He's out to get you for the Sandoe robbery, did you
know that? And also for robbing Mrs. Hedberg, did you
know that?"

"To think that there are swine like you in the world," said

Oscar quietly. "But if I should happen to tell the sheriff what kind of hoodlums you and Lif are?"

Rasmus' eyes filled with tears. He knew that the sheriff would never believe a tramp, and he knew that Oscar knew it too.

Liander laughed a harsh, nasty laugh. "Yes, you just go ahead and try it."

"A while ago you seemed a little worried yourself," said Oscar. "You were afraid that Mrs. Hedberg would revive and testify to one thing and another—that Anna-Stina has lied, for instance. Suppose the old lady revives, after all?"

"She won't," said Liander in a low voice. "After what has

happened here tonight I have a feeling that Mrs. Hedberg won't survive. Neither Anna-Stina nor we can take that risk."

Outside in the grass, Rasmus clenched his fists. Of all the gangsters in the world, Lif and Liander were the most ruthless. It sounded as if Liander had something horrible in mind when he said what he did about Mrs. Hedberg.

"You big fool, the whole thing is your fault," Liander barked. "Why did you have to go and stick your oar in? It will only serve you right when the sheriff locks you up. Don't take it too hard, though. Jails aren't so bad these days."

"You've probably spent enough time there to know," said Oscar, "and I'll do my best to see that you go back."

"Then you're a bigger fool than I thought," said Liander. "Don't you see that you'll get there faster if you try to stick us? If you have any sense in your head you'll get as far away from here as you can and keep your trap shut and never show your face around here again."

"No, and never have a peaceful moment when I see a cop," said Oscar bitterly. "If I could understand how skunks like you and Lif can exist! What a pleasure it would be to knock you senseless."

From his position outside the window, Rasmus nodded in agreement. How wonderful it would be if Oscar could mop up the floor with Liander. Oscar was as strong as a bull, much stronger than Liander. But Liander had his terrible gun which he was aiming at Oscar. If it hadn't been for that . . .

Next to him on the ground was an old board. Without really knowing what he was doing, Rasmus picked it up and banged it with all his might against Liander's right elbow. Liander let out a bellow of pain and rage as the gun flew in a curve over the kitchen floor. With a shout of triumph, Oscar hurled himself on Liander and they began to roll around on the floor. Rasmus watched, terrified, jumping up and down and biting his knuckles to keep from crying. He had never been able to stand seeing people fight.

This was no joke. Liander seemed to be just as strong as Oscar, and both men were grappling frantically for the gun. The gun! Rasmus suddenly came to life. Liander mustn't get hold of the gun!

As fast as his trembling legs could carry him, Rasmus ran around to the door and into the kitchen. The whole floor was shaking with the fight that was going on. The men were thrashing around so that Rasmus could hardly find a place to step. Liander's hand kept reaching out for the gun.

Rasmus kicked the horrible black weapon so that it flew into a corner. Then he picked it up with trembling hands, as if it were a poisonous snake. He could hardly bear to hold it, and he couldn't stand seeing and hearing those men thumping around and groaning and fighting.

Still holding the gun, he ran out to the kitchen steps. He wanted to be sick but he didn't have time. He just stood there crying, and saw how the strong wind lashed at the branches of the birch trees. The sun had just come up beyond the island, and was glittering on the crests of the waves. The seagulls had also started their day. They were circling over the old gray village and screeching as if they too were afraid. But probably only he was afraid, and so tired that all he wanted was to lie down and die. Oh, yes, one thing more.

He wanted to get rid of the gun. Sobbing, he ran over the cliffs. The wind was so strong that he could hardly stand up straight. When he reached the edge he flung the gun into the sea and a shiver of loathing went through his body.

As soon as he had done it he realized that it might have been the wrong thing to do. Oscar might need it to defend himself with. But it was too late now. The gun was down with the fish about thirty feet under water, and there it would remain for all eternity.

Rasmus dragged himself back from the edge of the cliff. There was Oscar, coming toward him with his clothes and hair in wild disorder, his rucksack on his back, grim and triumphant at the same time. Rasmus wanted to cry still more but he swallowed hard and forced back the lump in his throat.

"Come on, let's go," said Oscar.

"Liander?" asked Rasmus.

"Liander is taking a little nap by the fireplace. But where is Lif?"

"I locked him in the potato cellar," said Rasmus, exhausted.

Oscar looked at him with a broad grin. "The king of the fighters," he said. "You're not scared of anything, are you?"

"Yes, I'm terribly scared," said Rasmus, and he cried still more. Now Oscar would probably be angry with him and if Lif got out he would need the gun.

But Oscar wasn't angry. He only nodded and said, "Everything is all right the way it is. You and I probably aren't much good at handling guns anyway. But now we'd better get a move on and get out of here."

Rasmus moaned. He just *couldn't* get a move on. He looked pleadingly at Oscar. "There is only one thing I have strength enough for now, Oscar, and that is to sleep!"

11. Caught!

Rasmus was awakened by the familiar cackling of hens, that monotonous cackling which he disliked so intensely. He seemed to be back at Vaesterhaga again. Miss Hawk would be coming any minute to tell him he had to pull up nettles. Carefully he opened his eyes. Sure enough, there were two old hens strutting around him. They weren't white Vaesterhaga leghorns, though, but an unknown speckled kind. He was lying on a floor in a room where he had never been before. There was an open fireplace and in front of it sat Oscar, drinking coffee with a little white-haired old woman in a striped apron. They had poured their coffee out into their saucers and were blowing and drinking and talking away.

"I feel sorry for vagabonds who have to be on the road all the time," said the old woman kindly. "They can never get to heaven either."

"Now, now, Little Sara, you've got that all wrong," said Oscar. "You think that you'll go to heaven just because you sit at home by the fireside all the time. But you're mistaken there."

The old woman put a piece of sugar in her toothless mouth and looked slyly at Oscar. "You'll see," she said.

Rasmus stirred. He wanted Oscar to see that he was

awake. But it was the old woman who noticed it first. "I suppose you'd like a little coffee, too," she said and looked at him with a kindly, childlike expression. "Coffee and bread. You need to eat a lot of bread before you become a man."

Oscar laughed. "That one is a real fighter, I can tell you —the king of fighters is what he is. But he probably could use a little bread anyway."

Rasmus couldn't remember how he had got to Little Sara's house. He only vaguely remembered that Oscar had carried him and that the seagulls had fluttered about him, screeching.

His eyes wandered around the room, where the chickens were ambling about as if they belonged there. It was poor and messy and dirty but it was wonderfully comforting to be there with the three-legged coffee pot standing in the fireplace, looking so cosy.

Little Sara poured some coffee for Rasmus into a blue cup which had no handle, and cut him a thick slice of rye bread. "I'll give you butter some other time. I don't have any now," she said.

Rasmus took the bread. It was sticky and had a doughy dark line running through it, but he liked bread that was not too well baked, so it didn't matter. He dunked it in the coffee and it tasted very good.

"You certainly will go to heaven, Little Sara, because you're so kind to tramps," said Oscar.

Little Sara nodded.

"But now about the sheriff," Oscar said. "I would be grateful if you would take the letter to him as quickly as possible."

Little Sara scratched her head, which was like a little white ball of yarn. "But I won't talk to him," she said with a worried expression. "Not a word. I'll just hand him the letter and leave, because otherwise he will give me a lecture about moving to the poorhouse."

Oscar gave her shoulder a reassuring pat. "You don't have to say anything. Just give him the letter, and everything will be fine—we hope, at least."

Little Sara still looked worried. She was like a child, afraid of some unknown danger. "I don't want to do it but I'll do it just the same, because the pastor says that we should be good to the poor."

Oscar laughed. He didn't mind being poor. "Yes, Little Sara, you have to be good to me because I'm poor as a churchmouse."

Little Sara shook her head in a worried way. "But first I have to feed the hens," she said.

"Be good to the hens, too," said Oscar.

Little Sara called the speckled hens and disappeared through the door.

Oscar looked at Rasmus, who sat in his lumpy bed on the floor finishing the last of his coffee.

"Coffee in bed, that's really something," said Oscar. "But look what I've concocted while you've been lying there snoring. I've been writing a whole novel to the sheriff." He pulled out a paper covered with writing from his jacket pocket and handed it to Rasmus.

"Am I supposed to read that?" asked Rasmus.

"If you can," said Oscar.

Rasmus took it and began to read. Oscar didn't write very well, worse than he did himself.

I didn't do it, I'm innocent as a bride. No I didn't and you have to believe me. There were two real skunks who did the Sandoe job their names are Lif and Liander who live at the inn if they havent moved in on old Mrs. Hedberg. They are the same ones even though the maid lies and says it was me but I didn't do it, I'm innocent as a bride. But I stood outside singing "Every forest has its Spring" Ask Mrs. Hedberg if she is still alive but she probably isn't if she is going to get rid of Anastina. Otherwise she won't live long, Mrs. Hedberg I mean because these crooks have no shame. But I've taken care of the necklace and the money too, such a pile I've never seen before and now read on attached paper where I've hidden the loot. You have to get it there otherwise you'll lose it. Now Little Sara will come with this. I don't dare myself because no one believes a tramp but I'm going out on the road to be FREE because I'm innocent as a bride because I didn't do it.

Yours truly

Paradise Oscar

Dont let Anastina be alone with Mrs. Hedberg.

Rasmus folded the paper and gave it back to Oscar. "Where did you hide the money?" he asked.

"In a secret place. But don't ask me where. You may be the king of the fighters, but I don't want you mixed up in this mess more than necessary. I'll tell you some other time. But I've written it on the little piece of paper which I'm putting into the letter to the sheriff."

He'll tell me another time and another time I'll also get butter with my bread, thought Rasmus.

They settled down on the hill behind Little Sara's cottage to wait. Oscar didn't want to leave before he was sure that the sheriff had really got the letter. But Little Sara was certainly taking her time about it. Now she had been away four hours and Oscar began to be worried.

"Little old peasant women aren't much good as letter carriers," he said. "You never know what they'll do next."

But Rasmus enjoyed the rest. He had slept again for a while and they had eaten something. The sun was wonderfully warm and there was a delicious smell of sap from the pine trees that sheltered Little Sara's cottage from the winds. Rasmus was comfortable where he was, and Little Sara's cat was stroking himself against Rasmus in such a friendly way.

When he saw the cat he remembered his dream. He had dreamed that he had a cat, a black one, like Mrs. Hedberg's little kitten. All his life he had longed for a pet of his own, and so had Gunnar. They had talked about it often. In the dream Rasmus had given his kitten herring and potatoes. It was probably only cats in dreams who ate such delicacies. He laughed when he thought of how cute that kitten had been.

"What are you lying there laughing at?" said Oscar.

"I dreamed last night I had a cat," said Rasmus.

Oscar mimicked him. " 'I dreamed last night I had a cat.' I think you're lying there making up rhymes."

"Do you know what my cat ate?" Rasmus asked.

"Field mice, I hope," said Oscar.

"No, he only ate potatoes and fish, and he was so fat."
Rasmus giggled.

Oscar was quiet for a while and then he sang:

> "Believe me if you wish
> But potatoes and fish
> Is just a little kitten's—

"Dish," cried Rasmus, elated. "Oscar, that's almost a
song."

"Yes, it is a song," said Oscar, and he took out his accordion. He played through the little melody which he had
hummed, and while they continued to wait for Little Sara
they played and sang their song over and over again.

> "I dreamed last night I had a cat
> Who ate only potatoes and fish.
> Believe me if you wish,
> But potatoes and fish
> Is just a little cat's dish."

How easy it was to make up songs! Rasmus decided that
he was going to make up a lot—about cats and dogs and
maybe little lambs. Naturally it wasn't as exciting as "I
Cut His Throat from Ear to Ear" or "Have You Heard
the Terrible Happening?" But, after all, blood didn't have
to flow all the time! After the ghastly night with Lif and
Liander he had had his fill of terrible happenings.

At last Little Sara came back, looking very pleased with
herself. "The sheriff wasn't at home," she said with her

simple, toothless smile. "He was out arresting people. Such things can take a long time and I couldn't wait for him."

"But Little Sara, you did give the letter to one of the policemen?" said Oscar anxiously.

Little Sara shook her woolly head guiltily.

"And here we've been waiting for ages!" said Oscar. "What have you been doing all this time?"

"I've been hurrying," Little Sara assured him. "I only stopped by to have coffee with Flora Carlson."

"For four hours?" said Oscar.

"We had a few things to talk about," said Little Sara with dignity. She didn't want to hear any reproaches.

"Give me the letter," said Oscar. Rasmus noticed that he was annoyed with Little Sara.

Now Little Sara again got that guilty look. "That letter —I forgot it at Flora Carlson's," she said. "Was it important?"

She was standing beside her red-currant bushes, picking off withered leaves and acting as if she were doing something necessary and just didn't have time to think about such trivial things as letters.

Oscar sighed. "No, Little Sara, it wasn't so important. You'll probably get to heaven anyway. Everything is fine the way it is."

"I wrote that letter with my heart's blood," he said to Rasmus afterward when they were on their way to Flora Carlson's to try to get it back. "I can't write two such masterpieces the same day, so I hope Flora has it."

Flora Carlson's cottage was already in sight along the road. But they never got that far. Two policemen suddenly appeared before them as if they had shot out of the ground —the same two who had taken Oscar to the sheriff before.

Oscar was furious—more so than Rasmus had ever seen him. The policemen were treating him as if he were the world's enemy number one and not a harmless vagabond.

"Get the gun from him," said one of them. Then they rushed at him and searched him all over.

"I don't have a gun," Oscar shouted. "I never had one. I never even had a toy gun when I was a kid, although I cried and begged my mother for one."

Then they were taken to the sheriff's office and one of the policemen sat down and wrote about them on a piece of paper while the other one held on to Oscar as if he were about to run away. He didn't hold on to Rasmus, and that wasn't necessary because Rasmus was standing as close to Oscar as he could get. What a nightmare this was! Never a moment's peace, but having to be afraid of robbers and sheriffs and policemen in turn.

But Oscar wasn't afraid. He was livid with rage. "I want to talk to the sheriff," he shouted, and banged his fist in the table in front of the policeman who was writing.

"The sheriff is at a party. He won't be back at his desk until tomorrow," said the policeman who was holding him.

"At a party!" screamed Oscar. "And here I stand, innocent as a bride."

"We've heard all that," said the one who was writing— Bergson, the other policeman called him. "You believe your own lies. But this time you'll get what you deserve, thank heaven, because people like you shouldn't be loose."

Oscar groaned. He turned to the policeman who was

holding him and pointed to Bergson. "Can I call him a blithering idiot or is there a law against it?"

"You can just bet there is," said the policeman who was holding him. "Calm down now and tell us your full name so that Bergson can write it down."

"Oscar," said Oscar. "What's yours?"

"My name is Anderson, but that is none of your business. What is your last name?"

"That's none of your business. You can call me Oscar and there's no law against it either."

Anderson laughed. He seemed a bit more good-natured than Bergson, who frowned and said, "I don't like your tone. Please change it."

"Please go to the devil," said Oscar. Then he turned again to Anderson. "Are you sure there's a law against calling Bergson an idiot? But if I meet an idiot and call him Bergson, no one can get me on that, can they?"

The idea made him roar with laughter. Then he leaned over the table, looked Bergson straight in the eye, and said with emphasis, "Bergson! A real Bergson is what you are!"

Bergson got red in the face and turned to Anderson. "Put him in number two, and then the sheriff can teach him manners tomorrow."

Anderson looked at Rasmus. "What are we going to do with this one?"

Then Bergson said something so horrible that Rasmus could hardly believe his ears. "This is the kid that ran away from Vaesterhaga," he said. "We'll have to see to it that he gets back there."

A pit seemed to open in front of Rasmus, and all the

world's misery came rolling over him like a big black wave. He was going back to Vaesterhaga. Life was over. He had lost Oscar. They were putting Oscar in jail and sending him back to an orphanage where he didn't want to be. He just couldn't accept that.

For a moment Rasmus stood there staring at Bergson with terror-filled eyes. But there was no mercy to be expected from that quarter. He looked desperately around him for help. There must be a way out.

The sun streamed through the open window, like a broad golden band over the floor, and brightened up the dreary office. That was the road to freedom!

Without thinking, Rasmus leaped out, just like an animal who senses the danger of capture near. They

shouted after him but he didn't stop to hear what they were saying. Like a bolt of lightning he ran along the empty street. It was along this street that he had come riding with the milk cart yesterday. He ran heedlessly down the hill toward the dairy, like a frightened rabbit, hopping over the sun-warmed cobblestones without looking right or left. He ran blindly without knowing where he was going.

There wasn't a soul around. But at the dairy two people suddenly dashed out from a side street. Rasmus didn't notice them before he had almost run right into the stomach of one of them. The person in question grabbed him roughly by the shoulders.

"Slow down there. We'd like to have a little talk with you." It was Lif.

12. The Rescue

"Now we're *really* going to have a little talk," said Lif, and he quickly pulled Rasmus behind the high fence that surrounded the dairy. No one was around at this time of day. Rasmus was caught.

Lif shook him roughly. "Answer fast, otherwise I feel sorry for you. Where's your partner, the tramp?"

"The police have taken him," said Rasmus, so weary that he was hardly afraid any longer. They probably wouldn't dare to kill him anyway.

Lif and Liander looked at each other in horror. They seemed more frightened than Rasmus.

"So they've got him," said Liander. "Well, Hilding, you know who he'll blame. Now we have to get out of here fast."

Lif kept an iron grip on Rasmus. "Answer quick. Did your pal have the dough on him when they took him?"

Rasmus couldn't decide whether it was wiser to answer yes or no to that question, so he didn't say anything. But Lif kept shaking him as if he thought the answer had got stuck in Rasmus' throat and could be shaken loose.

"What have you done with the money?"

"He has hidden it in a secret place," said Rasmus. "And I don't know where."

"Hilding, we're in a hurry," said Liander nervously.

"Shut up," said Lif. "Of course the tramp will blame us but if we disappear it's the same as saying to the sheriff that we did it. No, this is the time to keep cool, calm, and collected as never before."

He turned to Rasmus. "Were you there when the sheriff cross-examined Oscar?"

Rasmus shook his head. "The sheriff hasn't done a thing to Oscar yet because he's been at a party all day."

Lif whistled and for a moment looked almost relieved. "Yes, of course. He must be at Mrs. Rosen's birthday party. That's just fine. He'll be at the inn all evening and won't have time to question anyone, and tomorrow it may be too late." He leaned toward Liander and whispered something in his ear which Rasmus couldn't hear. Then followed a long, whispered conference over his head. Finally Lif said, "Listen boy, how would you like it if we got Oscar out of jail for you?"

Rasmus looked at him, stunned. He wanted Oscar out of jail as much as he wanted to live, but that Lif and Liander wanted to help him was beyond belief. Was there some good in them after all? Maybe they felt sorry for Rasmus because he was all alone. Suddenly he felt sorry for himself too. When he thought of how lonely he would be without Oscar, tears came to his eyes and he mumbled, "It would be very kind of you if you got Oscar out."

Lif grabbed him around the neck. "Yes, we're awfully kind. But open your ears now and get this and remember what I'm saying, because you're going to go and tell it to Oscar."

Rasmus looked at him, terrified. "I can't. Then they'll catch me and send me back to the orphanage."

Lif became impatient. "You'll do as we say. When it gets dark tonight you'll slip in to Oscar. The lock-up is in a separate building in the sheriff's yard."

"But if the police are standing guard—" said Rasmus.

"They won't be. When they have locked Oscar up, he's on his own and you can talk to him through the bars in the back window."

Rasmus nodded. If it wasn't any worse than that . . . He was prepared to risk a lot for Oscar's sake.

"Tell him that we'll come and let him out tonight. Uncle Liander here is very good at opening locks."

"Don't blab so much," snarled Liander. "We'll come and get him, but on one condition."

"I'm getting to that now," said Lif. "We want that money back. We need a change of climate and that is going to be expensive, so we want the dough."

"But if Oscar doesn't want to?" said Rasmus anxiously.

"We'll give him the necklace," said Lif. "He can't say that we aren't being generous."

These men certainly didn't know anything about Oscar. They thought they could bribe God's best friend with a necklace! They thought he had stolen the money and the necklace from them just because he wanted everything for himself! No, they didn't know anything about Oscar.

"But suppose he doesn't want to anyway," said Rasmus.

Lif got annoyed. "I know the man is stubborn, but he can't be that stupid. Ask him if he wants to spend years in the jug. He is the one who is getting stuck for this, not us, tell him that. I'll make it my business to convince the sheriff. Besides, it isn't a question of what Oscar wants or doesn't want. You've stolen one gun from us but I still have mine, and I'll bring it along tonight, tell him that."

They gave Rasmus more instructions. He was to stay behind a woodpile at the dairy until evening. He was forbidden to show his face in the village and risk being caught. He was not to let anyone know that he knew Lif or Liander or Oscar.

"As soon as it gets dark, you'll go there," said Lif. "When you've done what you're supposed to, you'll come back here and wait for us. We'll come and get you at midnight tonight."

"But I'm so hungry," said Rasmus. He put his hand in his pocket and took out the money Oscar had given him. "Can't I go and buy some buns for this?"

"No, you can't," said Lif. "Give it to me!" He grabbed the coins and he and Liander disappeared.

Rasmus sat down behind the woodpile, terribly shaken. They were the lowest of thieves and were going from bad to worse the way they just kept on stealing. The Sandoe robbery was ugly, and stealing Mrs. Hedberg's necklace was still uglier. But to take *his* money—that was the meanest crime of all!

But he had misjudged Lif. After five minutes he came

back with a bag which he threw at Rasmus. "Here," he said. "Eat! And stay behind the woodpile. Don't you dare move before the time comes."

Then he disappeared. Rasmus watched him for a long time. Crooks certainly were strange. One minute they chased you like a wild animal and the next they came with buns. Hungrily he opened the bag and peered into it. There were five cinnamon buns at two cents apiece. That made ten cents. But there were also a lot of little sugar cakes and gingerbread cookies that Lif must have bought with his own money. For a moment Rasmus almost felt as if he liked Lif. At least he didn't need to starve to death in his prison. This little tight spot between the woodpile and the fence was a long, narrow prison walk to Rasmus, although it was open at both ends. A jail ought to be locked so that the prisoners couldn't get out. If he was going to sit in jail, he might as well do it properly.

He took wood from the woodpile and barricaded both entrances. Then he made believe that he was a prisoner in the Aelvsborg Fortress, just like the man in Oscar's song:

"Here behind the bars I languish,"
Sighed the prisoner in anguish.

But jail wasn't as bad as people seemed to think. As a matter of fact, Rasmus was quite contented.

There was a small knothole in the fence and he peeked out through it to see if any flower-bedecked gondolas would come gliding along. But all he saw was the empty cobblestone street. As he walked around the woodpile, he suddenly heard little faint cheepings and when he investigated he found a bird's nest between two logs.

"Oh," said Rasmus. "Oh."

In the nest were three adorable baby birds chirping.

They were little miracles and he stood for a long time looking at them, filled with wonder. He was the happiest of all
prisoners. But suddenly he remembered that he was
hungry. He sat down on the ground below the nest and
opened the bag. He was also thirsty. If he only had something to drink too!

There must be people who look out for the welfare of
fortress prisoners. A pitcher of milk was standing on the
gatepost at the entrance to the dairy! A careless maid had
probably come to buy milk and forgotten it there.

For a while Rasmus tried to reason with himself. How
thirsty did you have to be before you could take a little of
someone else's milk? In this heat it would only stand there
and spoil anyway. He didn't think that the owner of the
milk would mind if he rescued a bit of it before it curdled.

Cinnamon buns and milk tasted good. Sugar cakes and
milk tasted good. And gingerbread cookies and milk tasted
good. He was having a wonderful time behind the woodpile. He poured milk into the lid of the pitcher and
dunked the buns in it, and sometimes he would put his
mouth to the edge of it and drink. He didn't take more
milk than necessary to wash the food down. His conscience
hurt him when he drank, but at the same time he felt that,
since he was imprisoned here against his will by two dangerous hoodlums, it was more or less the duty of society to
supply him with milk.

He soaked some crumbs in milk and offered them to the
fledglings on his index finger. They pecked at his finger with
their tiny beaks and it felt so funny. He was a prisoner
pining away behind prison bars and they were his only

friends, the little fledglings. The rest of the world had long
since forgotten him, but the little birds cheered him up
with their chirping. They would share his imprisonment
until death.

He cried a little when he thought about it. Then he
wasn't a fortress prisoner any more, but Rasmus, and then
he cried still more and longed for Oscar.

Later that evening when he stood outside the lock-up
and heard Oscar's familiar voice behind the bars, he was
absolutely wild with grief and sobbed and whispered in
the dark, "Oscar, you have to let them get you out. I have
nobody but you."

"I know," said Oscar, "but you must understand that I
can't go in league with robbers. Can't you see that?"

Rasmus only cried and sobbed harder. "Yes, but we can
go on the road afterward. I haven't anyone but you,
Oscar!"

"No, I guess you haven't," said Oscar. "And that blasted
sheriff is at a party. But now I'm going to get hold of him
if I have to tear this place apart." He started to bellow at
the top of his lungs, "Come here, all Bergsons and idiots,
and listen to me. Come here before I tear this place to
bits. I want to talk to the sheriff!"

Rasmus was terrified when Oscar began to shout and
he started to look for a place to hide. Between the lock-up
and the sheriff's garden there was a little bridge which
served as a shortcut between the sheriff's yellow house and
his office. Rasmus crept down under it and sat there listening to Oscar's roars from the lock-up.

"I told you to get me the sheriff! Can't you hear me,

you deaf fools? I want to confess. Get me the sheriff, but be quick about it!"

The sheriff's yellow house was dark and his office was also dark. Maybe Bergson and Anderson had gone to the party too. In any case, no one came when Oscar shouted, and finally he screamed, "Blame yourself if I run away tonight."

Rasmus jumped when he heard it. Oscar was going to run away after all! That was wonderful news. It was all the same to Rasmus what happened to the money and the necklace as long as he and Oscar could be free on the road again.

Two hours later they were on their way. But behind them like two black shadows were Lif and Liander.

Lif had been right when he said that Liander was good at opening locks. It hadn't taken him more than a quarter of an hour to get Oscar out. During this time Lif had been standing guard. Rasmus had also been standing guard—with Lif's hard hand around his neck. There had been no policeman and no sheriff in sight.

"The police have only themselves to blame," muttered Oscar when they were slipping out of the village under cover of darkness. Everyone was peacefully sleeping as if there were no such things as robbers in the world.

But the inn was far from quiet. They could hear the accordion music from there as they stole along the quiet street down toward the town gate. They were on their way to Little Sara's cottage.

"Where did you hide the money, Oscar?" Rasmus whispered.

"You'll soon find out," said Oscar grimly.

They came to Little Sara's cottage, which lay hidden behind currant bushes and old apple trees. Little Sara was probably sound asleep, little realizing what a strange company was just now moving stealthily through her gate, past her cottage, up over the hill, and into the forest beyond.

After they had walked a short distance they came to a huge stone pile. No one knew what it was or how it had got there. If it was an ancient relic, it certainly didn't look like one. It was a huge pile of stones and nothing more.

When he came up to the pile Oscar stopped. He turned around and glared at Lif and Liander. "So you're still there, my little Sunday-school boys. I was afraid I might have lost you on the way."

"You shouldn't worry about such things," said Lif. "You won't lose us so easily." He was pointing the gun at Oscar, who winced when he saw it.

"Don't fire that thing. I don't like the noise."

"Not if you get that dough out in a hurry," said Lif calmly.

"Oh, dear me," said Oscar. "Where did I put it?" He pushed his cap back on his head and scratched his neck. "It was somewhere around here," he said with a broad gesture which included the whole stone pile.

"We don't intend to play hunting for treasure, if that's what you think," said Lif. Liander was so nervous he was shaking.

"Get it out and fast. We're in a hurry. Can't you get that through your head, you big ox?"

The sky started to brighten over the treetops, and in the pale dawn Liander's face looked ravaged and drawn. He took deep puffs on his cigarette and couldn't stand still. "Well, out with it," he roared.

Oscar sighed and turned to Rasmus. "The sheriff has only himself to blame now," he said. "You can be my witness that I did what I could."

"Yes," said Rasmus faintly.

He felt so terribly sorry for Oscar. What a miserable ending to have those gangsters get away with the money. The only consolation was that Oscar was to get the necklace and that they were going on the road again when all this terrible business was over. If Mrs. Hedberg didn't get well again, her daughter in America would still get her mother's beautiful emerald necklace. That was at least something to be pleased about.

Oscar climbed up on the stone pile. Lif and Liander followed closely behind and Rasmus thought they looked as greedy as a pair of jackals.

Rasmus also came along. He sat down on a stone as close to Oscar as he could get. He was trembling with cold. He didn't take his eyes off Oscar.

"This is the place," said Oscar, and he began to heave away the stones. He threw aside boulders, which came rolling down like an avalanche and made a terrible sound in the deep silence of the forest. Lif and Liander were standing right behind him, watching every move he made, hardly able to control their suspense. When he uncovered the familiar oilcloth package Lif and Liander threw themselves on it in one leap.

"There's your blood money," said Oscar contemptuously.

"Count it all," cried Liander. "He may have stolen a lot."

"You filthy scum," said Oscar and spat.

Lif gave Liander the pistol and started counting. He sat in the stone pile counting bills until Rasmus became dizzy. The necklace was lying there too, and Lif put it in his pocket.

"Don't worry about the necklace," said Oscar. "I'll take care of that as we agreed."

"I've changed my mind. I don't think you deserve an emerald necklace."

But Liander started to shout. "Give him the necklace, you idiot! Don't you understand that is the only way of shutting him up—to make him a partner? Give it to him!"

"Partner," said Oscar with disgust. "I don't intend to become a partner of thieves and bandits. But I'm going to have that necklace to give back to Mrs. Hedberg. Will you get that through your heads, you crooks?"

Lif and Liander looked at each other and suddenly there was an ominous silence.

"*Did you hear what he said?*" asked Lif. "We don't shut that one up by making him a partner!"

"No, you can drink poison on that," said Oscar. "I won't be your partner as long as I'm alive."

"As long as you're alive, no," said Liander and gave Oscar a look which made Rasmus shiver still more. "But there are better ways of shutting you up, you see."

He pointed the gun at Oscar.

"Don't shoot!" cried Lif. "You're crazy, Liander."

"I'm crazy if I don't," said Liander. "Here are two witnesses too many and I intend to let them stay behind in this stone pile." He raised the gun again.

But from Rasmus came a wild cry. "Don't shoot," he screamed, and threw himself against Oscar. "Don't shoot, don't shoot!"

There was a shot, but not from the pistol which was being aimed at Oscar. It came from another gun, and the bullet blew the pistol out of Liander's hand with such tremendous force that it flew across the stone pile.

"Oscar, are you dead?" cried Rasmus shrilly.

"No, I'm not dead," said Oscar. He looked out over the forest. Behind those dense pines must be the person who had fired the shot.

Lif and Liander stood there, pale and staring too. They got still paler when they saw two policemen coming toward them from behind the trees, with guns in their hands, running and jumping over the stones. The policemen came steadily nearer to the little group in the middle of the stone heap.

"I protest," shouted Lif when the handcuffs were closed around his wrists. "I protest! This tramp—this is the one you ought to handcuff. Just take a look at the package he had hidden in the rock pile!"

"You can save yourself the rest," said the sheriff, who also suddenly appeared and looked at Lif and Liander grimly.

Oscar grabbed him by the arm. "Sheriff, I swear I'm innocent as a bride."

The sheriff nodded. "Yes, Oscar, I've been standing behind that tree for the last half hour and I know that you're innocent as a bride."

13. A Dream Come True

"I don't understand a thing," said Oscar, still stupefied. He was sitting in the visitor's chair in the sheriff's own office and smoking a fine cigar which the sheriff had offered him from the box on the desk. "How did you manage to get there at exactly the right moment?"

Oscar kept on looking at the sheriff while he puffed on his cigar. Rasmus was standing behind Oscar's chair, breathing in the wonderful aroma of the smoke. But he wanted the sheriff to forget that he was there, so he was making himself as small as possible.

The sheriff had been so good to them. He had saved their lives and they had spent the rest of the night in his yellow house and his maid had given them breakfast. Now he was sitting behind his desk and had written down everything that Oscar had told him about Lif and Liander. Then he had offered Oscar a cigar. He was a good man—but he did have the power to send boys to orphanages, whether they wanted to go or not. So Rasmus tried to stay out of sight.

"I got your letter," said the sheriff. "Without that letter

we wouldn't have had Lif and Liander behind lock and key now."

"The letter?" said Oscar, amazed. "But you couldn't have got my letter—"

"Sure I did," said the sheriff. "I got it late last night. I was at a party at the inn and while we were sitting there having coffee they came and said that there was someone who wanted to talk to me outside. I sent a message saying that I was busy and couldn't leave. But I shouldn't have done that, because suddenly Flora Carlson came storming in like a wild creature."

"Flora Carlson," said Oscar. "I knew that it couldn't be Little Sara."

"No, Flora Carlson. That one knows what she wants, I can tell you. She handed me the letter as I was sitting at the table. 'You can't sit here collecting your big salary without doing anything,' she said. She had found the letter on the floor of her porch."

"Oh, that Little Sara . . ." muttered Oscar.

". . . and she knew it was important because she had read it. 'Now will you please do the rest, sheriff?' she said to me."

"Flora should get a medal," said Oscar.

"Yes, and you ought to have a medal too," said the sheriff. "I've probably been a little unfair because I believed what Mrs. Hedberg's maid said about the tramp who had threatened them with a gun. But as soon as I had read the letter I realized that you were innocent and I'm not so bad that I can't admit my mistakes."

Oscar looked pleased. "All's well that ends well," he

said. He blew out a puff of smoke, which Rasmus sniffed blissfully. Cigars smelled so gentlemanly. But he kept his eyes on the sheriff and didn't forget for a second about the orphanage, although the sheriff was telling them such exciting and interesting things.

The sheriff thanked Oscar because he had warned him about Anna-Stina. "I rushed off to Mrs. Hedberg as soon as I had read the letter, and I think I got there just in time. Last night she regained consciousness. I don't want to think the worst of that stupid Anna-Stina but it was probably a good thing that we arrested her when we did."

"Do you think that Mrs. Hedberg will get better?" asked Oscar eagerly.

"I certainly hope so," said the sheriff. "I went there to deliver her necklace a while ago, and you can imagine how happy she was."

"She'll probably give me a big tip the next time I sing for her." Oscar chuckled, and went on, "So Anna-Stina is locked up now?"

The sheriff nodded. "It was when we were going to lock her up last night that we realized you were about to run away. We followed you the whole time—Bergson, Anderson, and I."

"That Bergson is an idiot," said Oscar.

"Maybe," said the sheriff. "But he is one of the best shots in the country, which you perhaps had occasion to notice last night."

"Yes, never did an idiot come at a more convenient time," said Oscar. He got up. "Now I hope I'm free."

"Of course. But this brave little Vaesterhaga boy—" The sheriff looked at Rasmus.

Rasmus didn't wait to hear any more. It took him only a couple of seconds to get outside the door and start running for his life. But behind him he heard Oscar call, "Wait for me, Rasmus!"

He turned around and there came Oscar, running so that his rucksack bumped up and down on his back.

"Don't let him take me, Oscar," said Rasmus, panting, when Oscar had caught up with him. "I want to be with you."

"Dear me," said Oscar worried. "Soon they'll arrest me for kidnaping instead. Boys like you shouldn't be wandering around on the road."

"But it's only until I find someone who wants me," begged Rasmus. Deep down he didn't believe that himself. He felt almost as if he were trying to fool Oscar as he said it, because he didn't really think that he would ever find someone who would want him. But he was wrong.

After they had been walking the whole day, Rasmus began to be tired. "Where are we going to sleep tonight, Oscar?" he said.

Oscar kept trudging cheerfully along in the dust. He seemed to be able to walk any distance without getting tired. "We'll always find some place to lay our weary heads," he said.

"What a lot of different places I've slept in since I ran away," mused Rasmus. "Two nights in barns, one night on the floor of the empty cottage, one night at Little Sara's and one night at the sheriff's. I wonder where I'll be sleeping tonight. It's sort of exciting never to know ahead of time."

"Well yes, I suppose so," said Oscar.

Rasmus looked dreamily toward the red evening sky. "I wonder where I'll sleep all the other nights of my life?"

"Who knows?" said Oscar.

They walked along in silence for a while. The road was narrow and hilly and winding and had many gates and barriers. "I've opened sixteen gates today," said Rasmus. "I've kept count. Over there is another one, but it's already open."

"There have always been a lot of gates on this road," said Oscar.

"How do you know? Have you ever been here before?"

"Many, many times," said Oscar.

They walked through the gate. There was a sign nailed to the gatepost which Rasmus stopped and read:

> I always shut the gate when I go through,
> But oh, you lazybones, you never do!

"It seems to have been the lazybones who went through the last time," said Oscar. "Come, let's sit down for a while and take in the beauty of the landscape."

On the other side of the gate was a lovely little meadow with lush green grass and lots of flowers. Rasmus closed the gate properly behind him. At least nobody was going to be able to call him a lazybones. Oscar was already sitting in the grass among the bluebells and daisies, and Rasmus

threw himself down beside him. It felt good to rest his legs.

"If I were a cow I would stay in this meadow and refuse to budge," said Oscar. He scratched his head and said, as if to himself, "Isn't it funny that I'm unable to stay in one place but just have to keep on walking and walking? No matter where you go, it's about the same. Grass and flowers and trees and the sky and the forest and the moon and houses. So therefore I don't understand why I can't stay in the same place for any length of time."

"But it's fun to keep on walking," said Rasmus, "at least in the summer. But in the winter it's nice to have a house to live in."

"Yes, in the winter you get frostbite," said Oscar.

In the distance they heard the sound of horses' hoofs and carriage wheels, and Rasmus got up and ran to the gate as fast as he could. Who knows—maybe he could earn himself a tip. It was a carriage with seats both in front and in back, and a man was sitting alone holding the reins.

"This is Mr. Nielson from Sten Farm," said Oscar. "He's a good farmer."

Rasmus held the gate open wide and bowed deeply as the farmer drove through.

"What a polite little boy," said the farmer, holding in the reins. Then he caught sight of Oscar, who was sitting in the grass at the side of the road. "Well, well, there is Oscar. So you're around these parts again. It's about time!"

Oscar nodded. "Yes, I'm back. Can we ride along with you?"

"Yes, hop in," said the farmer.

Oscar and Rasmus quickly scrambled into the back seat and the carriage rolled on.

"Here's a tip for you," said the farmer, and he gave Rasmus a five-cent piece. Rasmus blushed with delight. It was just amazing how those coins had rained over him this last week since he found the first one at the ice house.

Rasmus glanced at the farmer. He looked kind and he wasn't old at all. His face was tanned and his eyes were very blue.

"Where did you find that boy, Oscar?" he said, pointing with his thumb over his shoulder at Rasmus.

"I picked him up on the road," said Oscar. "He's going to be with me for a while."

"Doesn't he have a mother who can take care of him?"

"No, he doesn't, poor thing."

Rasmus kept on staring at the sunset. He felt shy when people talked about him in his presence.

"If you want to know the truth, the boy has run away from an orphanage and now he is looking for a home."

The farmer nodded. "Yes, I thought it was that Vaesterhaga boy I read about in the paper yesterday." He turned around and looked at Rasmus in a friendly way. "Why did you run away from the orphanage?" he asked.

Rasmus continued to stare at the sunset and didn't answer. But when the farmer repeated the question he said quietly, "I didn't want to stay there."

Perhaps the farmer thought this was reason enough, because he didn't pursue the question.

The road had lots of curves and hills, and there were

still more gates, which Rasmus opened. At last they came
to a big hill which was so steep that Oscar and Rasmus got
out and walked beside the carriage.

"Now we're almost at Sten Farm," said Oscar. As they
walked up the hill they could see the farmhouse, high on
a hill. It was a beautiful red house, and the evening sun
shining directly on it made it look cozy and welcoming.

"Can't we ask if we can sleep there tonight?" Rasmus
asked Oscar.

But when they came to the fork in the road it was the
farmer himself who made a suggestion. "Do you want to
come in and have something to eat?"

"Do we, Rasmus?" asked Oscar teasingly.

"Yes, thank you," said Rasmus at once. Oscar had
taught him that you should never say no when food was
offered because you never knew where the next meal would
come from.

"I'll probably get something besides food—maybe a
lecture too?" said Oscar, looking at the farmer. But he
didn't get an answer.

A while later they were sitting at the big folding table
in the farm kitchen eating sausages and bacon with their
host. His wife poured Rasmus a glass of milk and gave
him bread with lots of butter. Then she laughed and said,
"This is the smallest tramp who has ever sat in my kitchen,
and believe me there have been many here."

Rasmus liked her at once. She had blond, curly hair and
a gentle, serious face, and she was pretty.

While Rasmus was eating he was listening to Oscar
telling them about Lif and Liander and Mrs. Hedberg's

necklace. "It will most likely be in the paper," said Oscar proudly. "Then you can read all about me and Rasmus, king of the fighters."

Mrs. Nielson was looking at Rasmus. She looked at him for such a long time that he finally turned his head away.

"Poor little thing," she said. "Weren't you happy at Vaesterhaga?"

Rasmus stared down into his plate and didn't answer.

"How are things at Vaesterhaga?" continued Mrs. Nielson. "We've been thinking of going there to look for a foster child, but we haven't got around to it yet. We should have gone this winter, but then I had some trouble with my arm."

"Yes, we just haven't got around to it yet," said her husband.

Rasmus raised his eyes from his plate and looked at Mrs. Nielson. "You would probably want a girl," he said shyly.

Mrs. Nielson smiled. "No, as a matter of fact we had been thinking about a boy because of the farm. Since we don't have any children of our own, we have no one who can take care of the farm for us later on."

"Yes, we did have a boy in mind," said the farmer.

"With curly hair," said Rasmus.

Mrs. Nielson looked at him in amazement and laughed. "Yes, how did you guess? I had pictured him with curly hair, I really had."

Rasmus nodded. "I understand," he said and chewed persistently on a bacon rind.

"But of course straight hair would be all right, too," said the farmer, and he playfully pulled at one of Rasmus' straight tufts of hair.

"Yes, it isn't the hair that counts, after all," said Oscar. "If I were you, I would take Rasmus, the king of the fighters, with straight hair. That is, if he wants to himself, of course."

Mrs. Nielson smiled at Rasmus. "Would you like that?"

Rasmus felt shaken. Was it possible that they wanted him? Could there really be someone in the world who wanted him?

"Would you like that?" the pretty lady had asked so casually. Would he like it! They were so kind and handsome, both Mr. Nielson and his wife, and they must be rich, too. The kitchen was so attractive, with copper pots on the walls and hand-woven rugs on the floor. The house was big, with many rooms, and they had two maids and a big red barn, so surely they must be rich. Rich and kind and handsome, and they wanted him!

"You can stay with us for a few days first, and then we'll see if we get along," said Mr. Nielson. "Perhaps this isn't something you decide on the spur of the moment."

"I'm sure I would like it very much," said Rasmus shyly.

"You'll never get a better boy," said Oscar.

Mrs. Nielson looked gravely at Rasmus. "Yes, I think I could become very fond of you," she said.

Afterward she served them coffee on the veranda, and then Rasmus was left alone with Oscar. It was only then that it dawned on him that now he would be separated from Oscar, and it came as a blow to him.

"Oscar," he said. "Do you think I ought to stay here?"

"Of course you should stay. You'll never find a better home."

Rasmus was quiet. In a way he had been hoping that Oscar would say something else—that he couldn't be without Rasmus, that the two of them belonged together. But he didn't say it. And of course Rasmus would be a nuisance when Oscar wanted to go on the road.

"You can walk much faster now when I'm not along," said Rasmus, and his voice trembled a little. "You can walk many more miles a day."

"Yes, of course I can," admitted Oscar. "But the miles are about the same, all of them, so it doesn't matter how far I walk."

Rasmus sighed. "I hope you won't meet any more gangsters when I'm not with you."

"Oh, there couldn't be that many around, and you bet I'll do all I can to stay clear of them."

Rasmus was quiet for a while and then he said, "When you go to bed tonight, you'll be all by yourself."

Oscar took Rasmus' hands in both of his. "Then I'll be by myself. That won't be easy for old Oscar. But it'll be nice for me to know that you're sleeping in a nice little room at Sten Farm tonight and all the other nights and that you don't have to roam the roads."

Rasmus swallowed hard. "Think if we never see each other again, Oscar."

Oscar was still holding his hands. "Of course we'll see each other. One fine evening when you're sitting in the kitchen having supper with your father and mother, there'll be a knock at the door and God's best friend will be standing there. And he'll say, 'I wonder if I may sleep in your hayloft tonight?' There you'll be, fat and happy, and you'll say, 'Of course.' Won't that be fun?"

But Rasmus didn't think that would be fun. His eyes began to get a glassy stare and Oscar continued. "Besides, I'll be coming around more often than you think. I promise you we'll see each other again."

"Honestly, Oscar?"

"As sure as amen in church. And think what fun you'll have with all the horses and cows and calves and pigs here."

"Do you think they have a cat here?" said Rasmus.

Mrs. Nielson came just then to get the coffee tray and overheard his question. She said, "No, we have no cat, because I can't stand them. But our dog had five puppies yesterday. We can go and have a look at them tomorrow."

Five puppies can make a little boy of nine forget all the sorrows in the world. Rasmus was overjoyed. Tomorrow would be a wonderful day.

"You're probably very tired now," said Mrs. Nielson. "I'll come right away and show you where you're going to sleep." Then she went out with the coffee tray.

"We'd better say good-by now," said Oscar. "I'm sleeping in the hayloft tonight and will take off early in the morning."

"But you'll come and see me soon," said Rasmus anxiously.

Somewhere within him a voice whispered that he would probably never see Oscar again, and that was a thought he couldn't bear. But he didn't want to think about it right now. He was so sleepy . . . and then there were the puppies he was going to see tomorrow.

He took Oscar's hand. "Thank you for letting me go with you on the road, and thank you for being so good to me."

"Thank you," said Oscar. "I think you're a fine fellow, even though you have straight hair."

Then Oscar left. Rasmus stood on the veranda watching with blurred eyes as he walked away in the twilight with his rucksack on his back. He went up the ramp to the hayloft and Rasmus saw him open the big door. Then he disappeared inside and Rasmus couldn't see him any more.

14. Homecoming

Rasmus woke up early the next morning. He knew that it was early because the sun that was streaming in under the dark blue roller shade was the early-morning sun and the sounds he heard in the house was morning sounds. Someone was banging around the iron stove down in the kitchen and someone else was grinding coffee.

Sleepily he looked around the room. It was a lovely little room and this was the softest bed he had ever slept in. Then he heard what he thought sounded like his new father and mother in the kitchen. He immediately recalled their kind faces. It was exactly the kind of father and mother he had dreamed about at Vaesterhaga so many times. Yes, it was a miracle. He had his own home and a father and mother at last.

But why wasn't he happy? Why, on the contrary, did he feel so terribly sad? The more wide awake he became the sadder he got, until finally he was more miserable than he had been since he ran away from Vaesterhaga. Something was tearing him apart inside. He was so miserable he thought he would die. He tried to think about the puppies he was going to see, but it was impossible when he was so sad.

Oscar! It was Oscar he was longing for so terribly. His heart ached so and there was only one cure. He had to find Oscar and talk to him, beg to be allowed to go on the road with him again.

But it was probably too late. Most likely Oscar had already gone. Rasmus could almost see him wandering along a distant road in the morning sun, far, far away. Oh, how would he ever live without Oscar?

With a cry he flew out of bed and began to put on his clothes. He was so unhappy and in such a hurry that his hands shook when he was trying to button his shirt and he had a hard time getting his pants on.

He met Mrs. Nielson in the doorway. Why did she have to come now? He didn't have time for any explanations. "I have to go and tell Oscar something," he mumbled and rushed by her.

"I think that Oscar has already left," she called after him. "I saw him come out of the hayloft a half hour ago."

Blind with tears, Rasmus ran down the stairs and out in the farmyard. He realized that Oscar must have left, but he just had to see for himself. He had to convince himself that there was nothing to hope for. Like a madman he raced over the farmyard toward the barn and up the ramp where he had seen Oscar disappear the night before. With a great effort he pushed open the big door to the hayloft. After the strong sunlight outside, it seemed completely dark. He couldn't see a thing and kept on sobbing, "Oscar, Oscar."

There was no answer and he began to cry out loud. Now his eyes had become accustomed to the dark and he looked around the desolate hayloft. They still hadn't started to bring in the hay at Sten Farm and the loft was as empty as a desert, and there was no Oscar.

Rasmus moaned. It hurt so much inside him that he couldn't stop. Terrible sobs racked his whole body. He leaned his head against the wall and made no effort to control himself.

Then he heard the door open behind him. Mrs. Nielson was probably coming to fetch him just when he needed to be alone. She mustn't hear him cry. He tried terribly hard to stop, but he couldn't. He was crying worse than ever. He was ashamed and hid his face in his hands. He leaned against the wall and let the tears run between his fingers.

"This is certainly a sad morning song," he heard someone say. But it wasn't Mrs. Nielson's voice—it was Oscar's! And there was Oscar standing beside him.

Rasmus rushed at him and clung to his arm. "Oscar, I want to be with you. You have to let me go with you!"

"Now, now," said Oscar. "Let's sit down out here in the sun and talk it over."

He pulled Rasmus outside with him. They sat down on the ramp with their backs toward the door and Oscar put his arm around Rasmus' shoulders.

"Look at this, Rasmus," he said, pointing to the farm. "Look what a beautiful farm you'll live on. In a little while they'll be leaving with the milk and you can go along. Then when you come home you can go and look at the new puppies and talk with your mother and father."

"I want to be with you, Oscar," sobbed Rasmus.

"Your very own father and mother—just think about that," said Oscar. "You have been looking for them for such a long time."

"But I'd rather be with you and go on the road. Can't *you* be my father?"

"A tramp for a father—how would that look? You don't want a tramp for a father." Oscar sounded almost angry.

"Yes, a tramp like you," mumbled Rasmus.

"But you've said all along that you wanted a father who is handsome and rich."

Rasmus turned and looked at Oscar through his tears. "I think you're quite handsome."

Then Oscar laughed. "Yes, as handsome as a bride, and rich too. The sheriff gave me ten dollars, so I'm rich!"

"But we don't need so much money to go on the road," Rasmus said. "And it doesn't matter if I get frostbite in the winter. I want to go on the road with you anyway. Please, Oscar!"

He couldn't say any more because now he was crying again.

For a long time Oscar was quiet. Then he put his hand on Rasmus' shoulder and said slowly, "Well, if that's what you want, that's the way it's going to be."

From Rasmus came a deep, happy sigh and slowly a smile lit up his tear-stained face. He pulled Oscar by the sleeve. "Come, let's go right away."

"No, first you have to go and tell Mrs. Nielson that you have changed your mind."

Rasmus looked anxious. "Must I? Couldn't you—"

"No, my boy, that you have to take care of yourself."

It isn't easy to tell people that you don't want them as parents, and for someone as shy as Rasmus it's a terrible ordeal. But Rasmus was prepared to do anything in order to be with Oscar.

He went over to the water trough in the barnyard and washed away all traces of tears from his face. Then he waved to Oscar to bolster his courage and took off toward the kitchen with determined steps.

Both the farmer and his wife were there having breakfast. Rasmus hesitated at the door the way tramps are supposed to. A wave of terror shot through him. Now he would have to begin explaining. What was he going to say? Would they be very angry?

"I'd rather be with Oscar," he mumbled.

At first there was a silence in the kitchen and then Mrs. Nielson said, "Come and sit down and tell us why you'd rather be with Oscar."

Rasmus squirmed. "I'm more used to him," he said quietly.

Mrs. Nielson wanted to push him over to the table but he resisted. He planted his feet firmly on the floor and struggled like a stubborn mule. He was so afraid that they would try to keep him from going with Oscar.

"You'll need some food in you if you're going on the road again," said the farmer, laughing.

"And you'd better hurry because Oscar is probably waiting," said Mrs. Nielson.

That didn't at all sound as if they were going to try to

keep him against his will. He stopped struggling and let himself be pushed over to the table. He cautiously sat down on the edge of a chair and looked uncomfortably at the two who were to have been his father and mother.

"Now we won't get any help with the puppies," said Mrs. Nielson.

Rasmus lowered his eyes. "I'd rather be with Oscar," he mumbled.

Mrs. Nielson stroked his cheek. "Don't look so sad," she said. "I guess we'll have to go to Vaesterhaga and see if we can find someone else to take care of the puppies."

Rasmus suddenly became so excited that he forgot his shyness. "I know who is the right one," he said. "You have to take Gunnar. He has straight hair, but otherwise he's okay. He is the best one there. I know all the children and Gunnar is best."

"And he doesn't want to go on the road?" said the farmer teasingly.

"No, he wants to be on a farm more than anything else. He likes animals so much. And he doesn't say bad words. Big Peter and Emil and almost all the others do. Gunnar is the best one."

"I guess we'll have to take a look at this Gunnar, then, since he is so good," said Mrs. Nielson, and she gave Rasmus a huge plate of cereal.

When he was about to leave he shook hands with them both. He looked at Mrs. Nielson with big, serious eyes. "Don't take a girl with curly hair," he said pleadingly. "Please take Gunnar."

Oscar and Rasmus started walking along the road that lovely, sunny summer morning. It had rained during the night and Oscar took big steps over the puddles, but Rasmus plowed right through them so that it splashed all around him.

"My feet feel so happy," he said when he saw the mud oozing between his toes. "I'm happy all over."

Oscar laughed. "Yes, it must feel good to have got rid of a large farm with horses and cows and everything."

Rasmus happily splashed through the next puddle. "Do you know what I've been thinking, Oscar?"

"No, but it's something wise and clever, I'll bet."

"I've been thinking that when you're on the road you really own everything you see."

"Well, in that case you haven't made a bad swap," said Oscar. "Not if you own all this," he said, pointing to the landscape which lay before them, freshly washed in the morning sunlight. He stopped for a moment as if to take everything in around him. "Gosh, how green and beautiful everything is at this time of year! No wonder I feel the urge to be on the road."

Rasmus skipped happily along beside him. "Everything belongs to us. The birch trees are ours and the sea is ours and the fields are ours and all the bluebells—and the road is ours and the puddles are ours."

"The puddles are yours," said Oscar. "One is enough for me, and I'll give that away too if I have to."

"But the houses aren't ours," said Rasmus, "because they belong to other people."

"We won't think about that," said Oscar. "The houses are ours too—one house at least."

Rasmus' face grew serious and he looked longingly at the little gray cottages they passed. "Yes, you and I ought to have *one* house," he said with a little sigh, "a house where we could live in the winter and not get frostbite."

"Yes, that would be nice," Oscar agreed.

But the sun was so warm and winter was far away. They didn't have to worry about a house yet.

They walked on and on, and Rasmus owned all the green fields and meadows and lakes he saw, but he didn't bother about the houses.

They left the settlement behind them and came into the deep forest. The sun filtered through the tall, straight pine trunks and the little pink bells of the twinflowers seemed to be ringing in the most beautiful day of summer.

"We're going to walk through the Sten Farm woods," said Oscar. "All these trees could really have belonged to you."

"But I'd rather be with you," said Rasmus, and he looked adoringly at Oscar.

Oscar looked at the happy, barefoot youngster running beside him, thin and long-haired, covered with mosquito bites, in patched homespun pants and a blue striped shirt which had long been in need of washing—a tramp from top to toe.

"Then I have a confession to make," said Oscar. "I want to be with you too."

Rasmus got red and couldn't say anything. It was the first time that Oscar had said that he wanted him. He felt

still happier, if that was possible. He took gay leaps over the puddles and felt as if he could walk any distance.

Soon they came to the other end of the woods and the road curved softly down toward a lake. There was a little gray cottage just like all the others they had seen, with a couple of apple trees and surrounded by a fence badly in need of repair.

Oscar stopped at the gate.

Rasmus laughed. "You're crazy, Oscar. Are we going to sing *here?*"

"No, we're going to sing as little as possible around here," he said as he walked toward the house. Rasmus followed him.

There was a woman standing with her back toward them, hanging up towels on a clothesline stretched between two apple trees.

"Martina," said Oscar. The woman turned around. She had a heavy, broad face and she didn't seem at all pleased to see Oscar.

"So here you are," she said.

Rasmus stopped a few paces away. This was obviously someone Oscar knew. But she wasn't very nice to him—in fact she was angry. She pointed at Rasmus. "Who is that?"

Oscar gave Rasmus an encouraging look. "Well, I've sort of acquired a son en route. But he's so small you hardly notice him around. His name is Rasmus."

The woman's expression didn't change, and Rasmus began to wish that they would get out of there.

"How have you been while I've been on the road this time?" Oscar asked her, and he sounded almost worried.

"What do you think?" said the woman. "I've worked like a dog and still I haven't been able to make ends meet. But of course that doesn't matter so long as you can be out gallivanting around the roads."

"Are you very mad at me, Martina?" said Oscar humbly.

"Yes, I am," said the woman. "I'm so mad I'd like to slap you." She was still for a moment. Then she did something amazing. She put her arms around Oscar's neck and

laughed and said, "Yes, I'm mad. But oh how glad I am to have you back home again!"

Rasmus stood there utterly confused and didn't understand a thing. Did Oscar live here? Was there really some place where Oscar actually lived? He had never pictured Oscar as having a home. Oscar was the wanderer, day in and day out, summer and winter. Oscar couldn't live anywhere. But if he did live here, who was this Martina? Was he married to this woman? Rasmus was standing beside the apple tree trying to figure it all out. The happy feeling had left him and he suddenly felt abandoned.

Oscar and Martina were looking at each other and laughing. It was as if Rasmus no longer existed. They didn't care about him. But suddenly Martina let go of Oscar and came up to him. She stood in front of him with her hands on her hips, big and broad, almost as big as Oscar. Her eyes were kind and happy. She laughed at him, but it was a kind laugh, as if something had struck her as being very funny.

"So, Oscar, you've gone and got yourself a boy on the road," she said, looking Rasmus up and down.

"Yes, he's a funny little fellow. Can you imagine, he wants a tramp for a father. He would rather have me for a father than Nielson at Sten Farm. What do you think about that?"

"If he wants you for a father he doesn't have much sense," said Martina.

"No, that's true. But if he got you for a mother he would be doing all right."

"This is quite sudden," said Martina. "But your crazy ideas are always sudden, Oscar. Doesn't the boy have any parents?"

"No," said Oscar. "He has no one but you and me."

Martina took Rasmus under the chin and lifted up his face so that she could see his eyes. She looked at him for a long time and then she said, "Would you like that? Would you like to live here with us?"

All at once Rasmus knew that it was exactly what he wanted. He wanted to live with Oscar and Martina in the little gray house by the lake. Oscar and Martina weren't handsome and rich and Martina didn't have a blue hat with feathers. But it didn't matter. This is where he wanted to be.

"Are you sure you want someone with straight hair?" he asked shyly.

Then she took him in her arms. No one had done that since the time he had an earache and had been allowed to sit in Miss Hawk's lap. Martina's arms were hard and strong, but still they felt soft, much softer than Miss Hawk's.

"Do I want a boy with straight hair?" said Martina laughing. "Yes, of course I do. I certainly wouldn't want a curly-headed one when my own hair is as straight as can be. One curly-head in the family is quite enough," she said, and she looked at Oscar.

Oscar was sitting on the steps playing with a little black kitten that was stroking itself against him. "A boy with straight hair or no one," said Oscar. "That's what we've always said, Martina and I."

Rasmus' eyes were sparkling and his whole face lit up.

"Rasmus," said Oscar, "have you seen this kitten?"

Rasmus ran over and sat down on the steps beside Oscar. He picked the kitten up in his lap and stroked him. "This is exactly the kind of kitten I dreamed about," he said.

"Then that's your kitten," said Oscar. "You know, Martina, Rasmus and I have composed a song about a cat who eats herring and potatoes."

"I have herring and potatoes on the stove in there. Would you like some?" said Martina.

Oscar nodded. "Yes, thank you," he said, and then he
sang in a thundering voice:

> "You can believe me if you wish,
> But potatoes and fish
> Is just a little kid's dish."

He took a firm grip on Rasmus' shoulder. "Come, let's go
inside."

Maybe Rasmus had been born in a little gray cottage
like this. Maybe his first days had been spent in a kitchen
like this with scrubbed wooden floors and a wooden sofa
and a folding table and begonias on the windowsill. Maybe
that is why it felt like coming home to him when he
climbed over the high threshold, worn down by so many
feet.

He was sitting with Oscar and Martina at the kitchen
table eating herring and potatoes. He was warm and happy.
He had come home. Martina was laughing and talking
noisily and it was hard to believe that it was the same
Martina who had been so furious before. He just couldn't
be shy with her because she made him talk whether he
wanted to or not. But it wasn't at all the same way grown-
ups used to talk to him—just to be nice. Martina seemed
to talk to him because she thought it was fun.

"That's the most insane thing I ever heard," she said
when they told her about Lif and Liander. "I'd like to get
my hands on those two."

"Ha, they'll probably get enough punishment anyway,"
said Oscar. "But I know who you do have to talk to! You

have to persuade the municipal authorities to let Rasmus stay here. I can't understand municipal talk. There's no point in my going because they'll only ask, 'What did you do last Thursday, Oscar?' "

"That's something I would like to know, too," said Martina. "I wonder what you were doing last Thursday when I was working in the parson's laundry until eleven o'clock at night."

And while she cut bread and put herring in front of them she talked about how hard it was to be married to a lazy-bones like Oscar. "You see, Rasmus, one fine morning I wake up and find Oscar gone and on the kitchen table is a note saying, 'I'm off again.' That's all. What do you think about that?"

Oscar didn't look sad at all, but continued to stuff himself with herring and potatoes and said happily, "Keep it up, Martina, keep it up."

"I don't know what else I can say when I've already called you lazybones," said Martina.

Then Rasmus intervened in Oscar's behalf. "Oscar isn't really lazy," he said. "He told me that he doesn't always want to work. But when he works, he works hard."

Martina nodded. "That's true. Do you know what Nielson said the other day? 'Oscar is my best farmer when he wants to be,' he said."

"Now I want to work," said Oscar. "I'm going to ask God to take some vagabond blood out of me in exchange for a little more farmer's blood." Then he looked at Rasmus and smiled slyly. "But just the same I think Rasmus and I will make a little tour, come spring."

Rasmus looked at him, his eyes full of admiration. How wonderful to have a tramp for a father! How wonderful to have God's best friend for a father!

"Let's take one day at a time," said Martina. "Tomorrow you're going to mend the fence and dig up potatoes, and the day after tomorrow you're going to Sten Farm and help bring in the hay."

Oscar nodded. "Yes, Nielson told me, so I know already. But tomorrow Rasmus and I are getting up early to fish for perch." He turned to Rasmus. "We have an old rowboat here. We'll row out to a place I know. Do you like to fish?"

Rasmus' face was radiant. "I've never done it," he said.

"Then it's high time you did," said Oscar.

Yes, it was wonderful to have a tramp for a father—and Martina for a mother. This was all he had ever dreamed of. Wasn't this what he had always said to Gunnar—that they should go out on their own and find someone who wanted them?

The thought struck him like lightning. Gunnar! He almost choked on the herring. If Gunnar really came to Sten Farm, he would see him! It was hardly a mile through the woods, and he could go with Oscar when he worked on the farm. He could see Gunnar's puppies and Gunnar could come here and see his kitten. Maybe Gunnar could come along fishing for perch sometimes.

"Of course," said Oscar when Rasmus asked him about it. "Gunnar can come fishing with us."

"And see my kitten," said Rasmus.

"And see your kitten," said Oscar.

Rasmus couldn't sit still. It's impossible to sit still when you're so happy. "At Vaesterhaga Gunnar used to say that the only animals we were allowed were the ones in our hair."

Martina laughed. "We don't want that kind around here," she said. "By the way, you're both filthy. Go down and throw yourself in the lake for a while."

Oscar sighed. "Now it starts," he said.

Rasmus went outside. What luck that he had a lake too! This was truly a remarkable day—the most wonderful of his life. He stopped on the porch and waited for Oscar. There was his kitten sleeping in the sun. Yes, it was a day of miracles. He had a lake and a cat and a father and a mother. He had a home. The walls of the cottage were worn and shiny, almost like satin. What a beautiful house it was! With a thin, dirty little hand, Rasmus lovingly stroked the walls of the house that was his home.